Secret in the Maple Tree

A Beka Book Reading Program

by Matilda Nordtvedt

illustrated by Frank Hicks

 **A Beka Book**
A MINISTRY OF
PENSACOLA CHRISTIAN COLLEGE
PENSACOLA, FLORIDA 32523-9160

Contents

Secret in the Maple Tree

A Beka Book Reading Program

by Matilda Nordtvedt

illustrated by Frank Hicks

A Beka Book

A MINISTRY OF

PENSACOLA CHRISTIAN COLLEGE

PENSACOLA, FLORIDA 32523-9160

Contents

A Beka Book ◥◣ Reading Program

Handbook for Reading *(grades 1–3)*
Primary Bible Reader *(grades 1–3)*
Read & Think Skill Sheets *(grades 3–6)*

1st
Fun with Pets
Tiptoes
Stepping Stones
Secrets and Surprises
The Bridge Book
Open Windows
Kind and Brave
Aesop's Fables
Strong and True

2nd
Story Tree
Treasure Chest
Hidden Treasure
No Longer a Nobody *(novel)*
Paths of Gold
Sunshine Meadows
Silver Sails
All Things—Even Frisky *(novel)*
Growing Up Where
    Jesus Lived
All Kinds of Animals

3rd
Paths to Adventure
Footprints
Crossroads
Pilgrim Boy *(novel)*
Secret in the Maple Tree *(novel)*
Better Bridges
Worlds of Wonder
Pilgrim's Progress

4th
Song of the Brook *(novel)*
Saved at Sea *(novel)*
Salute to Courage
Liberty Tree
Flags Unfurled
Trails to Explore
Adventures in Other Lands
    (Speed/Comprehension)

5th
Rosa *(novel)*
Noah Webster: A Man Who
    Loved Words
Beyond the Horizon
Windows to the World
Of America 1
Adventures in Nature
    (Speed/Comprehension)

6th
Billy Sunday
Message of the Mountain *(novel)*
Mountain Pathways
Voyage of Discovery
Of America II
Adventures in Greatness
    (Speed/Comprehension)

Introduction

S ecret in the Maple Tree is a delightful story based mainly upon the childhood experiences of Mrs. Ebertina Erickson Nordtvedt, the author's mother-in-law. The author chose the fictitious name, Hilda, to relate this story based upon Mrs. Nordtvedt's memoirs.

Hilda's parents were immigrants from Norway who came to the United States in the late 1800s. Norwegian immigration to the United States began in the 1820s with the arrival of the ship, the *Restoration*. The *Restoration* is often compared to the *Mayflower* because the Norwegian "pilgrims" were dedicated Christians who put God first and who wanted a better life for their families. After arriving in New York, most Norwegian immigrants settled in the North. They followed the waterways to the Middle West, to the Great Plains, and to the land beyond. Hilda's papa settled his family in Minnesota on a small farm. Hilda loved her life on the Minnesota farm, but she had to learn to accept necessary change and to trust God in all things. Her closeness to God through prayer was the guiding strength of her life.

The truly Christian family in *Secret in the Maple Tree* edifies the reader. Boys and girls enjoy the story's old-fashioned flavor tempered with modern appeal. All feel as if Hilda is a special friend and eagerly desire to read more about her.

Chapter 1
The Friendly Maple

Hilda carefully wiped the dishes that Papa had washed. Papa seemed happy tonight, and Hilda wondered why. He had looked sad so often since Mama went to heaven.

"You're a good dish wiper for an eight-year-old," Papa said as he put the dishes into the cupboard. Whistling a merry tune, he took the dishpan outside to empty it. Seventy-five years ago, when Hilda was eight, there was no plumbing on farms in Minnesota.

Hilda sat down at the kitchen table with her storybook from school.

"Read to me," begged four-year-old Lois, leaving the rag doll she was playing with to come and sit on a chair beside her older sister.

Hilda sighed as she looked into the little girl's round, blue eyes, so like her own. Hilda could read faster when she read to herself, but Lois loved stories and didn't know yet how to read.

"All right," Hilda said, putting the book between them so Lois could see the pictures.

Hilda read the story to Lois, then looked up at Papa, who was sitting at the other side of the table. Papa had a letter spread out in front of him, and he was writing on some paper. Papa hardly ever wrote letters.

"Did you get a letter from somebody?" asked Hilda.

Papa looked up and smiled at the two girls. "Yes, I did," he said, "a very nice letter."

"Is that why you were whistling?" asked Hilda.

Papa stroked his beard. "Was I whistling?" he asked. "I didn't know."

Hilda thought it strange to whistle and not know it, but everything about Papa was strange tonight.

"The letter is from a woman named Magda," said Papa. "I went to school with her in Norway. She married Pete Olson, and I married your mother. Now Pete and your mother are both in heaven—" Papa's voice trailed off.

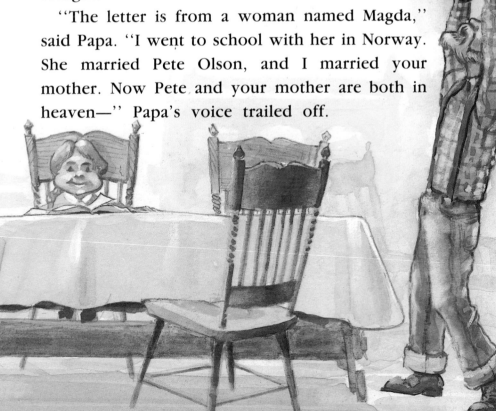

Hilda got a funny feeling in her stomach. She twisted the end of her long, blonde braid as she looked at Papa, waiting for him to finish.

Papa pushed back his chair, crossed his legs, and stroked his beard again.

"How would you like to have a new Mama?" he asked, "and a brother?"

Hilda's mouth dropped open. She stared at Papa.

"I want a new Mama and a brother," said Lois, running around the table to climb on Papa's knee. "When will they come?"

Papa looked at the calendar on the wall. "The letter says they can come anytime. I should leave for Illinois on Saturday to get them. The trip will take a week. The Petersons said you may stay with them while I am gone. Hans Peterson will do the chores for me here."

Papa began to whistle again. He stood up and threw Lois up into the air.

Hilda dropped her eyes to hide the sudden tears. She turned the pages of her storybook. The pictures blurred. Maybe Lois wanted a new Mama and a new brother, but she didn't. She wanted things to stay just as they were.

Papa had many things to do on Saturday morning before he boarded the train for Illinois. Hilda and Lois did the breakfast dishes all by themselves. While Papa was packing their things, Hilda slipped out to her favorite maple tree in the grove of trees behind the house. Her tree was easy to climb. Climbing to the spot where she always sat, she looked up at the clear, blue sky and began to talk to God.

She didn't have much time. Papa would be ready to leave any minute, but she had to tell God right away what was bothering her.

"Dear God," she began, "please don't let that lady come to be my new Mama. Make her change her mind, or make Papa change his mind—or something. I don't want a new Mama and a new brother. I want things to stay just as they are. Please, God."

Hilda felt better after she had prayed. She was sure that God would take care of everything.

Hilda would like to have stayed longer in the maple tree, but she knew Papa would be looking for her. With a last wistful glance around her, she jumped down from the tree and hurried to the house.

Papa was coming out with the suitcases. He put them into the wagon. Prince and Taffy, the horses, were already hitched to the wagon and eager to be off.

Shutting the door firmly behind him, Papa swung Lois up into the wagon. Hilda climbed in by herself. Papa tucked a blanket around them,

jumped in himself, clucked to the horses, and they were off.

Papa whistled all the way to the Peterson farm, where he let Hilda and Lois off with their suitcase. The girls kissed Papa goodbye and ran into the house. Mr. Peterson jumped on the wagon with Papa. He would ride to town with him and bring back the wagon and horses.

The Peterson house smelled of freshly baked bread. It had red and white checked curtains at the windows and potted plants. Hilda loved to go to the Petersons'.

Mrs. Peterson helped Lois take off her coat. "We're going to get a new Mama," announced Lois.

Mrs. Peterson laughed. "I know," she said. "I'm as happy as you are."

Hilda didn't look at Mrs. Peterson. Happy? She wasn't happy. Then she remembered her prayer in the maple tree and felt better. God would do

something to stop the new Mama from coming. Wouldn't He?

Mrs. Peterson's children were all grown up and gone, but she had some toys and games for the girls to play with. She let Hilda help her roll out sugar cookies and doughnuts. Hilda was so busy she didn't have time to think about the new Mama.

At bedtime, Mrs. Peterson read a Bible story to Hilda and Lois. It was about the prophet Elijah. When the wicked queen wanted to kill Elijah, God told him to hide by a little brook. Elijah lived there by the brook, and God sent birds to him every day with food.

Hilda liked the story. She would have enjoyed hiding by the little brook. That was something like her maple tree.

"But the brook dried up," went on Mrs. Peterson. "Then God told Elijah to go to a certain widow's house and stay there for a while."

Hilda frowned. Why did God let the brook dry

up? Why did Elijah have to leave the cozy spot for someplace else? Why did things always have to change? She thought about Papa's errand to Illinois. Having a new Mama would change everything. She didn't want things to change!

"Mrs. Peterson," she asked suddenly, "God always answers our prayers, doesn't He?"

Mrs. Peterson nodded. "He certainly does. Sometimes He says *yes,* sometimes *no,* and sometimes *wait.*"

Hilda smoothed out her dress over her knees and thought hard. "Why would He say *no*?" she asked, looking up at Mrs. Peterson.

"Because He knows better than we do what is best for us," she explained. "Sometimes we pray for things that would harm us more than help us."

In bed that night, Hilda thought about Mrs. Peterson's words. She had an uneasy feeling. What if God said *no* to her prayer about the new Mama? What if the new Mama came, after all?

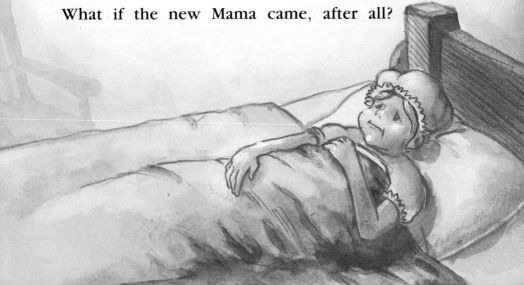

Chapter 2
The New Mama

The week at the Peterson farm flew by quickly. Papa was coming home on Saturday afternoon. Mr. Peterson would meet him in Willmar with the wagon. Hilda and Lois could go along if they liked.

Hilda was so eager to see Papa she almost forgot about the new Mama and brother until she saw them getting off the train with Papa. The new Mama was almost as tall as Papa. She had black hair smoothed back from her face and tied in a knot at her neck. Her eyes were dark brown and her cheeks rosy.

The boy with her had black hair and brown eyes like his mother. He was quite a bit bigger than Hilda, even if he was only one year older.

Hilda suddenly felt like crying. The next thing she knew, Papa had swooped her up in a big bear hug. She buried her face in his shoulder and

tried hard not to cry. It was so good to have Papa back, but why did he have to bring these strangers?

The new Mama gave Hilda and Lois each a kiss on the cheek and shook hands with Mr. Peterson. She told John to say *hello* to his new sisters, but he only stared at them. Mr. Peterson led them to the waiting wagon.

Mr. Peterson and Papa talked as they rode along in the wagon. Lois snuggled up to the new Mama and began to talk to her. John didn't say a word. Neither did Hilda. She had a lump in her throat that wouldn't go away.

Papa let Mr. Peterson off at his farm and then drove toward home. Nobody spoke. Even Lois seemed to have nothing more to say.

Finally, Papa broke the silence. "I should have had the house cleaned up better for you, Magda," he said as they pulled up at the door. He glanced at her. "Didn't think about that until this minute."

"Never mind," answered the new Mama quietly. "I'll clean it." She set her mouth in a firm line.

And clean it she did! She began even before Papa had the fire going in the kitchen stove. Everybody scurried around at her brisk commands.

"John, shake these rugs."

"Hilda, find me some scrub rags."

"Lois, you pick up your things and put them in this box."

Papa soon left for the barn, mumbling that he must do the chores. Hilda knew it was too early to do chores. Papa just wanted to get out of the way of the new Mama's broom and scrub rag. Hilda wished she could get out of the way, too, but she didn't dare!

The new Mama looked almost fierce as she went after the dust and dirt. She had a frown on her

face, and her dark eyes snapped. Hilda knew she wasn't going to like the new Mama. She was bossing everybody around already. Oh, why had Papa brought her to live with them? She didn't like John, either.

Finally, the kitchen, living room, and downstairs bedroom were all dusted and scrubbed. "The upstairs will have to wait until Monday," said the new Mama, looking around at her work.

Hilda looked around, too. She had to admit that everything looked nice and smelled clean.

The new Mama went to the cupboard, took out cornmeal, and began to make cornbread. While the cornbread was baking, she took out bacon from the cooler to fry. Oh, how good the cornbread and bacon smelled!

Papa came in from the barn with the milk. He looked worried until he saw his new wife's face. She was smiling now.

"Supper is almost ready," she said. "I'll use some of that milk for cocoa to go with the cornbread."

"It looks right nice, Magda," said Papa, setting down the milk pails and stroking his beard.

"I hate dirt," said the new Mama, as she measured milk for the cocoa. As if they didn't know!

Papa whistled as he washed his hands in the basin. He even combed his hair.

Hilda felt all mixed up inside as she sat down at the table. She didn't want a new Mama, but the new Mama surely could make the house look nice. And she surely could make good food! Hilda had never tasted such delicious cornbread before!

After supper, Papa opened the family Bible and read a Psalm: "O give thanks unto the Lord, for he is good."

Papa closed the Bible and began to pray. He thanked God for the new Mama and for John and prayed that they might be a happy family together.

Hilda wasn't ready to say *thank you* to God for her new Mama and brother. Not yet.

When Papa finished praying, Mama started talking about heating water for Saturday night baths. While the water was heating, Mama did the dishes and made up a bed on the sofa in the living room for John. Before Hilda knew what was happening, she found herself in the round washtub in the curtained-off part of the kitchen.

The new Mama scrubbed Hilda's back and checked her neck and ears. Hilda felt good when she jumped out of the tub to dry herself.

The new Mama handed her a flannel nightgown. It had pink and blue flowers on it, long sleeves, and a ruffle around the neck.

"For me?" asked Hilda.

The new Mama nodded. "I made one for Lois, too. They'll keep you warm and cozy."

Hilda put on the new nightgown. How soft it felt against her skin! She looked up at her new Mama. "Thank you," she said softly, and slipped upstairs to bed.

Chapter 3
New Brother

Hilda didn't see much of John on Sunday. After church, Nels Larsen's mother asked John to come over to spend the day with Nels. The Petersons invited Hilda, Lois, Papa, and his new wife home for dinner. Mrs. Peterson insisted they stay for supper as well, so they didn't get home until it was almost time for bed.

Hilda wondered on Monday how she would feel walking to school with her new brother. She didn't like him very much. He hardly talked to her and never smiled. But go with him she must. John didn't know the way to school, so Hilda would have to show him.

The new Mama handed them their lunch buckets and hurried them out the back door. Hilda

pulled her coat collar up around her neck. The April air was cool.

They walked along in silence for a while. Finally, Hilda spoke up. "Did you go to school in Illinois?" she asked.

John looked at her scornfully. "Of course!" he retorted. "Do you think I lived out in the woods or something?"

Hilda felt the blood rush to her cheeks. It was a stupid question, but she was only trying to be friendly. He didn't have to be so mean about it. She opened her mouth to say so, but John was already talking.

"Illinois is a lot better than dumb old Minnesota. We have trees and hills and—"

"We've got trees, too!" retorted Hilda, thinking of their lovely grove behind the house and her own special maple tree.

"Humph!" snorted John. "Here there are trees only by the farmhouses. In Illinois we have trees all over the place. All I can see here is fields, fields, fields. I hate it!"

Hilda felt quite insulted by John's outburst. She thought her home was the most wonderful place in the whole world. How could John talk that way?

"I don't hate Minnesota," she answered stoutly. "I love it."

"That's because you don't know any better," sneered John. "You've never been any other place."

Hilda tried to think of a good answer to that, but she couldn't. She was glad they had come to the Larsen farm, where Nels and his older sister, Marie, would join them. At least for now the subject would be dropped.

Hilda fell into step alongside Marie. Marie was trying to learn her spelling words and didn't have time to talk. Hilda didn't want to talk, anyway. She wanted to think. She had to be ready to answer John the next time he talked about Minnesota like that. She'd tell him to go back to Illinois then if it was so much better. She'd tell him she didn't want a new brother, anyway.

Hilda didn't feel very happy having such thoughts, but it was all John's fault for being so mean in the first place.

Hilda's best friend, Louise Nelson, came running out of the schoolhouse as they drew near. She linked her arm in Hilda's.

"I heard about your new brother," she said. "He's walking with Nels, isn't he?"

Hilda nodded, looking at the boys, who were quite a ways behind them. Suddenly, she felt proud to have a new brother.

"Pete says he's going to show him who's boss the very first day," went on Louise. "Sounds like he's planning to beat him up."

Hilda's eyes blazed. "He can't do that!" she said hotly. "Not to *my* brother!"

Louise shrugged. "You know Pete. He'd do *anything.*"

Hilda marched into the schoolhouse and put her lunch pail on the floor of the cloak room. Then she took off her coat and hat and hung them on a hook above her lunch pail.

Ed Swenson began to ring the bell for Miss Dahlen, the teacher. Hilda took her seat. She felt uneasy. What if Pete really did what he said he would? What if he hurt John? Even if he didn't like Minnesota, he was her new brother, and she didn't want him to get hurt his first day at school.

Hilda breathed a sigh of relief when John and Nels came into the schoolhouse. Miss Dahlen

seemed to know John was coming. She had a seat ready for him next to Nels.

Hilda tried to learn her spelling, but she kept thinking about what Pete had said. She glanced back at him just in time to see him aim a spitball at John on the other side of the room.

John looked up quickly when the spitball hit his cheek. His dark eyes flashed as he looked around to see who had thrown it. Pete laughed. Hilda saw John clench his fists. She knew the fight had begun.

Everyone hurried out of the schoolhouse at recess time, even Marie, who usually stayed in to read or help Miss Dahlen. Hilda held on to Louise's hand. She felt scared. Pete was so much bigger than John! What was he going to do, anyway?

It didn't take long to find out. Pete, a head taller than John, was the school bully. He had

already pushed John flat on the ground. It was all John needed! Jumping up, he sprang at Pete like an angry animal.

But John was no match for Pete. Pete pushed him down on the ground again and was ready to pounce on him when something struck him from behind, taking him off guard. It was Hilda, crying and angry, who had come to her new brother's rescue.

"You leave him alone!" she screamed, as she grabbed Pete around the waist to keep him away from John.

Before Pete could push her away, Miss Dahlen appeared. "Children! Children!" she scolded. "What a way to act in the schoolyard!" She turned to Hilda. "Whatever has gotten into you?" she exclaimed.

John picked himself up and dusted off his pants. Hilda, still crying, let go of Pete and ran to Louise.

She was just as surprised at her actions as Miss Dahlen was. What had gotten into her to make her attack Pete? Well, at least she had stood up for her new brother. Maybe now he would be friends.

But John had no intention of being Hilda's friend. On their way home from school, after the Larsen children had turned in at their place, he looked at Hilda with a scowl.

"Let me take care of my own fights, will you? I don't need any *girl* helping me!"

Hot tears stung Hilda's eyelids. She thought he'd be pleased that she stuck up for him. But he wasn't.

Hilda tossed her long braids and walked faster. He could walk alone. She didn't care. She didn't like him one tiny little bit!

Frowning angrily, Hilda marched into the house. Suddenly, she forgot to be angry. Her frown disappeared as she looked around her. The kitchen was somehow full of sunshine!

Then she saw them, the new fluffy yellow curtains at the windows. Why, their kitchen looked as nice as the Petersons' now! No, it looked even nicer!

Six loaves of freshly baked bread cooled on the table. The new Mama sat busily knitting in the rocking chair by the cook stove. She smiled at Hilda. "Would you like a slice of fresh bread with sugar on it?'' she asked. "Help yourself. I think it's cool enough to cut.''

Hilda almost forgot about her quarrel with John as she munched the fresh bread and looked around at the cozy kitchen.

"I like the new curtains ever so much," she said shyly. "They remind me of sunshine.''

The new Mama looked pleased. "I guess we could all use a bit of sunshine," she said, glancing at John, who had just come into the kitchen with a scowl on his face. The fresh bread didn't taste as good now that Hilda remembered his angry words.

"Where's Lois?" she asked, suddenly noticing that she wasn't there.

"In the barn with your Papa," answered the new Mama.

"I think I'll go out there, too," said Hilda, suddenly feeling very lonesome for Papa.

"Change your clothes first," the new Mama said.

Chapter 4
Secret in the Maple Tree

Hilda found Papa in the barn mending a harness. Lois was playing with the kittens in the haymow. Hilda sat down on a feed sack, tucking her legs under her, and began to tell Papa about the events of the day. She was sure he would be as angry as she was when he heard how John had treated her after she stuck up for him.

To Hilda's surprise and dismay, Papa didn't agree with her when she insisted that John was mean and ungrateful. He just let her talk until she didn't have anything left to say.

"You finished?" he asked, looking up from the harness.

Hilda nodded.

"It's good for you to talk about it and get it off your chest," Papa said, "but really, Hilda, John acted like any boy would. You see, we men like to fight our own battles."

Hilda just stared at Papa.

"We men don't like to be bossed by the womenfolk. John feels like that, too, even if he is still only a boy."

Hilda couldn't believe her ears. Papa was sticking up for John instead of for her!

"*She* bosses *you*," Hilda said, pointing in the direction of the house, "and you don't care."

Papa stopped working on the harness, frowned thoughtfully, and stroked his beard. "Waal," he said at last, "that's a little different. She can have her way around the house. But when it comes to other matters—" Papa didn't finish his sentence, but Hilda knew what he meant.

"And I don't want my girl being sassy to her Papa, either," he said, sternly for Papa, and turned his attention back to the harness.

Hilda hung her head. She drew a circle on the dusty barn floor with her shoe.

"I'm sorry, Papa," she said at last. Then she turned and walked swiftly out of the barn. Tears blinded her eyes as she ran to her maple tree in the grove. Nobody understood her, not even Papa. She'd climb her tree and tell her troubles to God. He'd understand.

But this time it didn't help. Hilda told God how mean John was and how even Papa didn't understand and how she didn't want a new Mama. But today God seemed so far away. She found herself wondering if He was even listening.

A noise under the tree startled her. She looked down. There stood Lois, holding one of the kittens.

"Know what?" Lois said. "Mama made gingerbread for supper. I'm not to tell, 'cause it's a s'prise. And she let me lick the bowl."

"Gingerbread?" echoed Hilda, her mouth beginning to water.

Lois nodded. "And she told me about when she was a little girl and how her Mama died when she was little like me."

"Did she really?" asked Hilda slowly.

Lois nodded. "Yup, she did."

Lois skipped away from the tree. "I'm going in the house. Why don't you?"

"In a minute," promised Hilda. She watched as her little sister ran to the house. Lois never grumbled about anything. She was thankful for the new Mama, for little things like getting to lick the gingerbread bowl and hearing a story of long ago.

Suddenly Hilda knew why God seemed so far away. He didn't like her grumbly prayers. He wanted her to be thankful, as Lois was.

For a little while, Hilda looked at the sky and thought hard. Then she said, "Dear God, I'm sorry for grumbling. Thank you for Papa, even if he does stick up for John, and thank you for Lois. Thank you for the yellow curtains and the gingerbread and my maple tree."

Even as she said the words, Hilda felt happier. She slid down from her tree and hurried toward the house. She felt as if she had learned a secret in the maple tree. When you feel grumbly, if you say *thank you* to God instead, the grumbly feeling goes away.

Chapter 5
The Cakewalk

John wasn't the only newcomer to school. Just a week after he had arrived, Valerie showed up. Valerie had long red curls, dancing brown eyes, freckles on her face, and dimples in her cheeks. Hilda thought she had never seen such a charming girl. She and Louise claimed her at once for their special friend, even if she was a year older than they.

Sometimes the children played baseball during the noon hour, sometimes "Run Sheep Run" or "Hide-and-Seek." One day Valerie said, "Let's do something different. How about a cakewalk?"

None of the other children had ever heard of a cakewalk, but it sounded like fun. "How do we play it?" asked John, who seemed to enjoy being around Valerie.

Valerie puckered up her lips and looked about her. "We have to find a place to do it," she

said. Pointing to an old house off to one side
of the school, she asked, "Who lives there?"

"Nobody," answered Hilda.

"Good!" exclaimed Valerie. "We'll cakewalk in
there. Come on, let's go."

The children eagerly followed their new leader,
even John, Nels, and some of the other boys.
The house was old and tumble-down, but that
didn't bother Valerie. She squeezed through the
partly open door, and the rest followed her. The
house was empty of everything but dust and
cobwebs.

"Perfect!" Valerie said when they came into
the room that had been the parlor of the house.
"Now, everybody get a partner."

John blushed when Valerie took his arm, but
Hilda could see he was pleased. She turned to
take Louise for her partner, but Valerie stopped
her.

"No, no," she said, "your partner must be a
boy." She looked right at Nels until he shyly took
Hilda's arm. Soon everyone had a partner.

"We're supposed to have cakes to give away
when the music stops, but we don't have any,
so we'll skip that part," said Valerie. "Now do
as I do. Keep time to the music."

Valerie led the way around the room, humming
a catchy tune and keeping time with her feet.

The others followed. Hilda thought it was great fun. Round and round they "cakewalked" until they heard the school bell ringing in the distance. Everybody ran as fast as he could out of the old house and into the schoolyard.

Hilda's heart pounded from running so fast. She slipped into her seat and took out her arithmetic book. With a sigh she began to do her sums. Too bad the noon hour couldn't be longer. Cakewalking was fun.

That night as she snuggled into her bed beside Lois in the little upstairs bedroom, Hilda thought about Valerie and all of her new ideas. She wondered if they would cakewalk tomorrow and who her partner would be. With these thoughts running through her mind, Hilda drifted off to sleep.

The next day Hilda ate her lunch as quickly as she could. Still chewing on her apple, she ran outside with Valerie, John, and a number of other children. Laughing together, they raced to the vacant house, where they paired off and began the cakewalk. This time Carl walked with Hilda, and everybody hummed along with Valerie. Sometimes they laughed aloud and shouted.

The noon hour passed too quickly. How dull arithmetic seemed to Hilda when she got back to school!

The cakewalking continued all week. On Friday,

Hilda noticed a horse and buggy stop out in front of the vacant house. She saw Thor Brye lean out of the buggy and listen. Then he rode on toward the schoolhouse, stopped, and went in.

When the children came into the schoolhouse, Mr. Brye was still there. Hilda remembered that he was on the school board.

After all the children were in their seats, Miss Dahlen stood up and said, "Mr. Brye has an announcement to make."

Mr. Brye cleared his throat before he began to speak. "I understand that of late your behavior during the noon hour has not been what it should be," he began. "Something resembling dancing has been going on in the vacant house." He pointed to it with his chin and cleared his throat again. "You know that dancing is against our

Christian beliefs. From now on you must stay on the school grounds during your free time except when the teacher excuses you to go to the ponds to skate."

Mr. Brye nodded to Miss Dahlen, then walked slowly out of the schoolroom. Hilda watched him go and then looked around at the glum faces of the other children. She felt glum, too. They hadn't been doing anything wrong. Why did Mr. Brye have to spoil their fun?

That night as Hilda lay in bed she thought about it. Had they done wrong to cakewalk in the old house? It had been such fun while it lasted. Hilda sighed. It was all over now. No use to fret about it. She would say her prayer and go to sleep.

Her prayer! She hadn't talked to God for a week! Each night she had been thinking about the cake-walking and who her partner would be. So that was it! Such things shut God out. Is that why Mr. Brye thought it was wrong?

Hilda wasn't sure, but as she closed her eyes to pray, she asked God to forgive her for forgetting about Him for a whole week, and to help her never to take part again in anything that shut Him out of her life.

Hilda felt happy and close to God as she snuggled into the covers and went to sleep.

Chapter 6
Secret Visit

Hilda missed Valerie. She hadn't been to school for two days. As Hilda worked on her spelling words on the second day, a plan formed in her mind.

If she asked the new Mama if she might visit Valerie, she would probably say no. So she wouldn't ask. She would simply stay and help Miss Dahlen after school for a few minutes, and then run over to Valerie's house on the way home. She would tell the new Mama she had stayed after school to help the teacher. That wouldn't be a lie.

Miss Dahlen smiled when Hilda offered to help her. "You may wash the boards and dust the erasers," she said brightly.

Hilda did the work as quickly as she could. When she had finished, she didn't offer to do more. "Goodbye, Miss Dahlen," she said, as she grabbed her coat and empty lunch pail and hurried out of the school.

Hilda's heart pounded with excitement as she

neared the house where Valerie lived. Valerie's folks were different from the rest of the people in the community. They never went to church. They ran a business in Pennock and only lived in a farmhouse because there were no empty houses in town. Louise told Hilda that her Mama said Valerie's folks always went to parties on Saturday nights in Willmar, and that's why they couldn't get up for church on Sunday mornings.

Hilda felt shy as she drew near to the white farmhouse. Maybe she shouldn't have come. Maybe she should go back before anyone saw her.

The door swung open even before Hilda knocked. There stood Valerie in her flannel nightgown. She threw her arms around Hilda.

"Oh, I'm so glad you came," she squealed. "I'm sick and haven't been anywhere for so long. It's dull staying home all the time." She led the way into the house.

"Are you alone?" asked Hilda, looking around her curiously.

Valerie nodded. "Mother has to help Daddy at the office. I get so lonely. I'm so glad you came." She squeezed Hilda's hand.

Hilda followed Valerie into the parlor, where there was a bed made up on the sofa. She looked in wonder at the shiny new linoleum floor, grey with pink flowers in it.

Valerie sat down on the bed. "What have you been doing at school lately?"she asked. "Tell me all about everything. Is Pete behaving himself? Does John miss me?" She giggled, and the dimples in her cheeks showed.

"We all miss you," said Hilda. "No, Pete isn't behaving himself." She sat down on the edge of a chair and began to tell Valerie everything she could think of that had happened at school during the last few days.

Suddenly tired, Valerie lay back on her pillow and pulled the covers over her. "Let's look at magazines," she said, pointing to a stack of them beside her bed. "Mother said I shouldn't be up."

Hilda picked up the pile of magazines and sat down on the bed near Valerie. She opened one of the *Ladies Home Journals* and looked at it, fascinated. She had never seen such magazines before. The only magazine that came to their

house was a Norwegian paper called *Folkebladet,* and it had few pictures. She gasped in admiration as she turned the pages and saw the large pictures of fancy ladies.

"Let's pretend these are picture albums," she suggested, "and these fancy ladies are our relatives. I'll come to visit you first, and you show me the albums. Then it'll be my turn."

The girls had so much fun at their pretend game that time passed quickly without their noticing it. Suddenly Hilda looked up at the clock on the parlor wall. It was almost five. She jumped up.

"I've got to go home!" she gasped.

"Don't go," begged Valerie. "It's so much fun having you here."

Hilda hesitated, feeling sorry for her friend but afraid to stay longer.

"Come back tomorrow, please?" Valerie pleaded.

"I'll try," said Hilda. "But I've got to go now. Goodbye, Valerie."

Hilda ran all the way home. When she burst into the kitchen, the new Mama was setting the table.

"Where have you been?" she demanded. "I've been worried about you."

"Didn't John tell you?" Hilda asked, not looking at the new Mama. "I stayed after school to help

Miss Dahlen. I cleaned the boards and —'' Her voice trailed off.

''Well, tell her not to keep you so late next time,'' said the new Mama crossly. ''Wash your hands now and finish setting the table.''

John gave Hilda a funny look when he took his place at the table across from her. His eyes seemed to say, ''You didn't tell the whole truth. You're up to something.''

Hilda squirmed and dropped her eyes to her plate. She felt uneasy with John looking at her like that. Did he know she went to see Valerie?

Hilda tossed her long, blonde braid back over her shoulder. She hadn't done anything wrong— just stopped to see Valerie after she'd helped Miss Dahlen. John needn't act so wise and know-it-all.

The next day Hilda stopped to see Valerie, but she didn't stay so long. The new Mama didn't seem to mind that she came home from school an hour later than John.

When Hilda stopped to see Valerie the third day, she found her friend with red spots on her face.

"Valerie!" she exclaimed, "you have red spots on your face up by your hair!"

"Do I?" asked Valerie. "Maybe I've got the measles or something. I hope you won't catch them."

"I had measles last year," replied Hilda.

"Daddy and Mother are going to ask the doctor to come out to see me today," Valerie said.

Hilda sat down on a chair and smoothed her dress over her knees.

"What happened at school today?" asked Valerie. "Tell me all about it from the very beginning."

Valerie snuggled down into her covers. She seemed to want to listen rather than talk today. Hilda didn't feel much like talking, either. She felt tired and a little hot. But she tried to tell Valerie what had gone on at school that day. Suddenly a noise startled them.

"Somebody's coming," said Valerie.

A loud knock on the door made them jump. Hilda was too frightened to move, let alone go to the door.

The door opened, and in walked a large man. Hilda jumped up and ran to him. "Oh, Dr. Ness," she cried, "I'm so glad its you!"

The doctor, smiling at Hilda, put down his black bag and took off his coat and laid it over a kitchen chair. "What are you doing here?" he asked Hilda.

"Just visiting Valerie," answered Hilda. "She's right in here."

The doctor took one look at Valerie and turned to Hilda. "Does your father know you're here?" he asked.

Hilda shook her head slowly. "I—I just stopped in on my way home from school."

The doctor frowned and turned his attention to the girl on the sofa. After examining her he shook his head. "Just as I thought—smallpox!"

Smallpox? Hilda's heart almost stopped beating. That was a terrible disease!

The door opened. Valerie's mother, who was red-haired and pretty like Valerie, burst in and hurried to her daughter's side. She gasped when she saw the red spots on Valerie's face.

"Smallpox," said the doctor gravely. "Have you folks been vaccinated?"

Valerie's mother shook her head.

"Then you must keep Valerie in a separate room from you. Otherwise you'll get it, too. You probably already have gotten the germs."

He turned to Hilda. "I don't know what to do with you, young lady, now that you've been exposed. If I take you home you'll infect your family."

"She could stay here," offered Valerie's mother.

"Oh, goody!" squealed Valerie. "Please stay, Hilda, we'd have such fun!"

Hilda's eyes filled with tears. She shook her head. Suddenly she wanted to be at home more than any place in the world. "I want to go home," she said quietly.

The doctor looked serious. He turned to Mrs. Shannon. "Perhaps it is the best," he said. "Thank

you for your offer, but if you and your husband also get the disease it wouldn't be good to have an extra one to care for.''

Dr. Ness gave Valerie's mother instructions as to how to care for Valerie, and then led Hilda out of the house and into the waiting buggy. He carefully tucked a heavy blanket around her, clucked to the horses, and they were off.

Hilda felt so sorry about what she was bringing home to her family that she wiped tears from her eyes and sniffed all the way home.

It was beginning to get dark when Dr. Ness guided the horses into the Johnson yard. He turned to Hilda before he jumped out of the buggy. ''You stay here a minute while I talk to your folks. They may want me to take you back to Shannons'.''

Hilda couldn't keep back the sobs when she heard that. More than anything, she wanted to stay in her own home. But maybe her family didn't want her, now that she was carrying the dreaded smallpox germs. Oh, why had she gone to Valerie's in the first place? She didn't know it would cause all this trouble.

In a few minutes, the back door opened and the doctor stepped out. Hilda could see the new

Mama framed in the doorway. Her words came clearly out to the buggy.

"Nonsense! I'll take care of her. Of course we want her here. I'll get the room ready right away."

Hilda was so happy to hear the new Mama say that, she cried harder than ever.

It never took the new Mama long to do things. In a few minutes, Dr. Ness was bringing Hilda into the house and up the stairs to the bedroom, which was to be Hilda's home for the next few weeks.

The new Mama didn't say much, just bustled around to get the room ready. Dr. Ness sat down beside the bed after Hilda had climbed in. "How long were you with the Shannon girl?" he asked.

Hilda knew she must tell the whole truth now. If only she had been truthful in the first place and asked the new Mama if she could visit Valerie, this might not have happened.

"I've been visiting her every day after school for three days," she whispered, her eyes filling with tears.

The doctor shook his head. He examined her and then turned to the new Mama. "I'm afraid she's coming down with it. Let's get the rest of you vaccinated. I only hope it's not too late."

Dr. Ness and the new Mama walked downstairs, leaving Hilda alone and very unhappy.

Chapter 7
Hilda Learns About Forgiveness

Two days later, Hilda broke out with red spots all over her face and body. The new Mama, coming into the room with her food, gasped when she saw her.

"So it is smallpox!" she exclaimed. "Just as I feared!"

Hilda expected a scolding from the new Mama, but she didn't scold. She simply busied herself around the room making Hilda as comfortable as possible.

"You'll be lonely up here by yourself, Hilda," she explained, as she turned to leave. "Smallpox is very catchy. I'm the only one who can come up here, and I must be very careful to change

my dress and wash my hands each time I do. I keep my dress out in the summer kitchen so it won't infect things in the house."

The new Mama started down the steps. "I'll be back up after a while," she said over her shoulder.

Hilda wanted to call her back to tell her she was sorry for making so much trouble. But the new Mama was already down the steps and in the kitchen. Hilda heard the door shut behind her.

Burying her face in her pillow, Hilda began to cry. It was terrible having smallpox! It was awful being stuck up in this room all alone without anybody! But even worse than this was the guilty feeling Hilda had. She had done wrong, and now she was causing trouble to everyone in the family.

Hilda thought wistfully of her maple tree out in the grove behind the house. How she would like to be sitting on her favorite branch right now, looking into the blue sky! Then maybe she could talk to God about her trouble. Somehow, He seemed so far away in her gloomy room.

If only she could see Papa—or Lois. Papa probably was angry with her for bringing home the dreaded smallpox. Oh, dear, why had she gone to visit Valerie? Hilda sobbed softly into her pillow.

She must have fallen asleep, for the next thing she knew, the new Mama was standing by the bed with a tray of food for her lunch. Hilda didn't feel hungry, but she was very glad to see the new Mama. It was so lonely with nobody to talk to! She sat up and took the tray.

Suddenly, she remembered what she must say to the new Mama. It was hard to get the words out, but she finally managed. "I'm sorry," she said, and then burst into tears. One tear rolled right down her face and off the tip of her nose into the bowl of potato soup on the tray.

The new Mama patted Hilda's head. "Now, now, don't cry. You'll only get worse."

Hilda cried all the harder.

"What's the matter?" asked the new Mama, gently, sitting on the edge of a chair near the bed.

"I'm—I'm making you so much trouble," sobbed Hilda. "You—you must be angry with me, and Papa must be, too."

The new Mama laughed. "Nonsense," she said. "Of course we're not angry with you. We forgave you before you even said you were sorry."

Hilda stared at the new Mama through her tears. "I thought you would punish me," she said, "or at least scold."

"Being sick is enough punishment," said the new Mama. "Now eat your soup. You need something in your stomach to help you get well."

Hilda took a few spoonfuls of soup. The new Mama stood up and fussed with the curtain at the window, trying to keep the bright light out. The doctor had told her the room should be partly darkened.

"It's funny about forgiveness," the new Mama said as she came to pick up the dishes when Hilda was finished. "Jesus said that if we don't forgive one another, He won't forgive us. When we think of how much He has forgiven us, it shouldn't be hard to forgive each other."

She patted Hilda's head and helped her snuggle back down into the covers. "Now don't you worry about a thing except getting well," she said.

Hilda listened as the new Mama walked down the stairs. She heard the door close and knew she would be all alone again for several hours. But this time she didn't cry. She thought about what the new Mama had said.

Forgiveness is a funny thing—you have to give it in order to get it. The new Mama said it wasn't hard to forgive people when she thought about how God had forgiven her.

Hilda closed her eyes and thought hard. Did she have somebody to forgive? John, who made fun of Minnesota and teased her? How about Pete? Could she forgive him for being so mean to John and everybody?

"Jesus, help me to forgive," she whispered, "and please forgive me for going to visit Valerie without asking."

A good feeling came into Hilda's heart. The room didn't seem so gloomy any more. She could talk to Jesus here just as well as in the maple tree! She knew He had heard her prayer, and He did what she had asked Him.

Hilda sighed and curled up under the covers. She wasn't really alone after all. Jesus was with her.

Chapter 8
Secret Visitor

The days dragged by, and Hilda stopped feeling so sick. But her face, hands, and body itched where the pocks were healing. The new Mama brought up a basin of lukewarm water and a soft rag.

"Don't scratch your face," she said, "or you'll get ugly scars. When the itching gets bad, dip this little rag into the water, squeeze it out, and lay it on the itchy place. It will help."

It did help. The new Mama changed the water often. Hilda kept busy carefully washing the itchy places.

Hilda could hardly wait to get well and back with her family and friends. It seemed as if she had been in the upstairs room forever. She had seen nobody since she got sick except the new Mama and Dr. Ness, who came to visit her every few days.

One afternoon when Hilda felt that she couldn't stand to be cooped up for one more minute, she heard a strange noise. It sounded like someone tapping on her window.

Hilda got out of bed and pulled back the curtain. John's grinning face startled her.

"I brought you something," he said. "Open the window a little wider."

Hilda pushed up the window and put a stick underneath to hold it up.

John held out a handful of prairie flowers. "Here," he said. "I thought you'd like some to look at since you can't come outside."

Hilda took the small bouquet of yellow and purple flowers and buried her face in them joyfully. "Oh, thank you!" she exclaimed. "I love them!"

"How long are you going to stay up here, anyway?" asked John. "I'm getting tired of having nobody to play with."

"Oh, John, you shouldn't be here," whispered Hilda, suddenly remembering. "You might get smallpox."

John shrugged. "I'm not scared," he said carelessly.

"How did you get up here, anyway?" asked Hilda.

"I dragged a ladder over from the barn. Papa went to Petersons' on an errand, so I figured nobody would stop me."

"Oh, John, you shouldn't have!" exclaimed Hilda, half scolding him and half praising him for doing such a daring thing for her. "You'd better put it back quick, or you'll get in trouble. Someone might see you. I think the doctor is coming today."

John shrugged carelessly, but started down the ladder. Hilda stayed at the window and watched him jump from the ladder and drag it back to the barn. Then she walked slowly to her bed and sat down. She felt good inside.

John wanted to be friends, or he wouldn't have brought the flowers. He had called her father "Papa" instead of "Mr. Johnson" as he used to. That made him seem like a brother.

Should she call the new Mama just plain "Mama" as John and Lois did? The new Mama had been so kind to her during the long, lonely days of her smallpox. Could she accept her as her Mama at last?

Hilda heard the kitchen door open and Dr. Ness's voice. He and the new Mama were coming up the stairs. Quickly she lay down and pulled the covers over her.

The doctor seemed pleased when he had looked Hilda over. "I believe you are well, young lady," he said.

"You mean I can go downstairs and back to school?" asked Hilda, sitting up. She could hardly believe her ears.

The doctor nodded. "And thanks to your good nurse here, you won't even have any scars on your face."

"Mama's the best nurse in the whole world!" said Hilda, suddenly feeling a surge of love for her. There, she had called her "Mama." It wasn't hard.

Mama smiled at her.

"Some of the folks in the community haven't had such good care," said the doctor. "You have done an excellent job, Mrs. Johnson."

Mama looked pleased. She turned to Hilda. "You wait here and I'll bring up some water for a bath. Then you must put on clean clothes. We'll hang your nightgown and bedding out on the

line to air before we wash them. Papa can burn the straw mattress, and I will wash the bedstead and the room."

"Very fine," said the doctor. "I wish the people in every home were so careful. Then the germs would not spread." He turned to Hilda and chucked her under the chin. "Be a good girl now," he said as he left to go downstairs with Mama.

A half-hour later, Hilda, scrubbed from head to toe and dressed in clean clothes, walked down the stairs. Her legs felt wobbly, but she was so happy! What fun it was to be in the kitchen again. The yellow curtains at the windows were prettier than ever. And there were Papa and Lois! She ran to hug them. Mama and John stood by, watching and smiling. Suddenly, Hilda ran to Mama and hugged her, too. Mama squeezed her tight. Hilda saw that Mama had tears in her eyes—happy tears.

John brought the checkerboard. "Let's play a game before supper," he said.

Chapter 9
A Secret to Share

School was out for the summer, but not many days later Bible school started. A young man from Minneapolis came to help Pastor Lunde teach the children.

Hilda liked Bible school. She wanted to learn more about God and the Bible. She felt good inside when she heard about His love and care for her.

Last summer Lars Fadum had been the teacher. Hilda would never forget him. He was such a good teacher. Hilda remembered the day that he had told them the story of Jesus dying on the cross for the sins of the world. Hilda had heard the story many times before, but this time it seemed different.

"It was because of our sins that He had to die," explained Mr. Fadum. "Because Jesus paid for our sins, God can now offer us forgiveness. He won't force this forgiveness on anyone, though. Each one must ask for it himself. Each one must himself invite Jesus to come into his life and give him eternal life."

Hilda felt uneasy when Mr. Fadum talked like that. She thought of all the times she had been bad. Would Jesus forgive her for all of that and come to live in her? Mr. Fadum said He would, but she must ask Him.

Hilda could hardly wait for Bible school to be over that day. She ran home as fast as she could and took refuge in her maple tree.

"Please, God," she prayed when she was seated on her favorite perch, "forgive me for the bad things I've done. Please, Jesus, come into my life to be my Savior and Friend."

Hilda felt so happy after she had prayed! She knew God had forgiven her; she knew Jesus had come into her heart. He would be with her always and would take her to heaven someday.

Hilda didn't tell anybody about her special talk with God in the maple tree. It was her own wonderful secret just between herself and God.

When Lars Fadum didn't come back to the Bible school the next year, Hilda was disappointed. Hans Berg, who was studying at the seminary to be a preacher, came instead. Mr. Berg was nice, but Hilda didn't think he was as nice as Lars Fadum.

One day, Mr. Berg told all the children to bow their heads while he asked them a very important question. "Just because your parents are Christians doesn't mean you are," he said. "If you are to be a true Christian, you must ask Jesus *yourself* to forgive your sins and come into your life. How many of you have done this?"

Hilda couldn't resist peeking. A number of children raised their hands. Mr. Berg then explained to the rest how they could receive Jesus as their very own Savior, but Hilda didn't listen. She felt a little cross. Yes, she had invited Jesus into her life, but she wouldn't raise her hand. It was none of Mr. Berg's business whether she was a true Christian or not. It was *her* secret, and she didn't intend to tell anybody. Why should she?

In a few minutes, Mr. Berg dismissed the class. Hilda hurried out of the church without a backward glance. She noticed a horse and buggy coming down the road in front of the church. As it came closer, she saw Valerie with her father and mother.

Valerie's father stopped the horses, and Valerie jumped out. She threw her arms around Hilda.

"I came to say goodbye," she said tearfully. "We're moving to New York."

Hilda couldn't believe her ears. "When?" she asked sadly.

"Tomorrow or the next day. As soon as Father and Mother get everything ready. I will miss you so much. Will you write to me?"

"Of course I will," said Hilda, "but you must give me your address."

"I don't know my new address," said Valerie, "but I'll send it to you when I find out."

Valerie hugged Hilda again and waved to the other children standing around watching. "Goodbye, all of you. Come and visit me in New York." She hopped back up into the buggy and waved again as her father slapped the horses and they started trotting down the road.

Hilda felt sad as she walked slowly home. She hadn't seen much of Valerie since Bible school had started.

Mama was behind the house cleaning new lettuce from the garden when Hilda reached home.

"Oh, Mama," she cried, "do you know what? Valerie and her parents are moving to New York."

Mama stopped washing the lettuce, wiped her hands on her apron and stared at Hilda. "You don't say!" she exclaimed.

Hilda nodded, feeling rather important to be

bringing Mama the news, even if it was sad news.

"And I never got over there as I intended to," Mama sighed, as she started washing the lettuce again.

Hilda looked at Mama curiously. Why should she go to see Valerie's mother? Mama was so plain and old-fashioned and Mrs. Shannon so fancy with her upswept hair and stylish clothes.

"Why did you want to go to see Mrs. Shannon?" blurted out Hilda.

"Because she doesn't know the Lord," Mama answered. "I wanted to tell her how much He means to me."

Mama sighed again and looked sad as she rinsed off the lettuce and took it into the house.

Hilda walked slowly to her maple tree, thinking hard. So Mama had a secret, too, but she didn't want to keep it to herself. She wanted to share it.

Hilda climbed her tree and leaned back amongst the branches, looking out at the blue, cloudless sky. She thought about Valerie: pretty, gay, rich, lively, and fun, but not a Christian. What good

was it to have all these other things if you didn't have Jesus? What could be better than having forgiveness and eternal life? What could compare with having Jesus as your very best Friend?

Suddenly Hilda knew that some secrets were to be kept but others to be shared. The one about Jesus in her life she should share, so others could have Him, too. Was there still a chance to share with Valerie?

Hilda jumped out of the maple tree and ran to Mama. "Mama," she blurted out, "Valerie said they were leaving tomorrow or the next day. Maybe there is still time to go to see them."

Mama was taking bread out of the oven. She didn't answer until she had the loaves standing in a fragrant row on the table.

"I think we should try," Mama said. "If they were on their way to town when you saw them, they probably won't be home until late. How about tomorrow morning before Bible school?"

"Good!" cried Hilda, clapping her hands together. She couldn't wait to see Valerie again and to share her secret with her.

The next morning after breakfast, Mama and Hilda started out for the Shannons' house. Hilda carried a jar of rhubarb jam to give them, and Mama carried her Bible. As the white house came into sight, Hilda began to feel uneasy. How could she tell Valerie her secret? It was so hard to put into words. But there was no other way for Valerie to know. Her heart pounding, Hilda marched up to the door with Mama.

Mama knocked. Nobody came. She knocked again. Still no answer. Then Hilda knew they were too late. The Shannons must have already left for New York. They had gone before Hilda and Mama could share their wonderful secrets with them.

Mama and Hilda sat down on the back step to rest. Hilda felt sad. She knew Mama felt sad, too. For a few minutes they just sat there, looked out across the sunny fields, and thought. At last Mama broke the silence.

"I think I know how Peter in the Bible felt when he said he didn't know Jesus," she said with a sigh.

Hilda didn't answer. Her mind flitted back to her meeting with Valerie in front of the church the day before. Suddenly she remembered something. Valerie had promised to write to her.

Hilda jumped up. "I know, Mama," she cried. "We can tell them in a letter. Valerie promised to send me her address."

Mama stood up. She seemed relieved. "That's a good idea, Hilda. Maybe we will get another chance." She took the jar of jam from Hilda. "Hurry, now, and run to Bible school," she said. "You mustn't be late."

Hilda hummed a little tune as she ran down the road to the church. She felt so much better knowing that she could share her secret after all. And some time today she must tell Mr. Berg her secret. It wasn't the kind of secret to keep to oneself. It was the kind to share. He would be happy to hear it.

Chapter 10
Fat Rats and Chicken Couples

Hilda, John, and Lois were playing hide-and-seek. Hilda was "it." She finally spied John in the barn high up on a stanchion.

"I see you!" she called.

"Sshh," he whispered as he motioned for her to come up where he was.

Hilda swung up on the stanchion beside him.

"Oh, you scared them away!" John said in dismay.

"What did I scare away?" asked Hilda.

"The rats. I was watching two of them playing by that hole."

"Let's be quiet and maybe they'll come back," Hilda said.

The two children kept very still, and sure enough, the rats came back, not two this time, but three.

"I didn't know there were such big rats in the barn," said Hilda. "Why don't we feed them and have them for pets?"

"All right," agreed John. "You go get some food while I wait here. But don't let Lois know. She'll tell."

It was Hilda's second secret with John. Quietly, she jumped down from the stanchion and ran to the house. Mama was taking a nap, so nobody saw Hilda take the bread and cheese and hurry back to the barn.

From their perch, John and Hilda dropped bits of food to the rats below. A fourth one came out, and they fought over the food. It was great fun to watch.

Every day, as soon as they had finished their chores, John and Hilda made their way to the barn with the scraps of food they had managed to collect. The rats became so used to the children, they didn't even run away.

Hilda and John decided to give them names. Two would belong to John and two to Hilda. Hilda decided on "Samantha" and "Jennifer," names she'd read in a book at school.

John scoffed at such silly names. Besides, he was sure his were *boy* rats. "Mine are 'Ole' and 'Oscar,'" he said.

"I wonder if we could teach them to do tricks," Hilda said.

"Sure we can. Tomorrow I'll bring a string and try something."

The next morning at breakfast, Papa said, "Children, I want you to stay out of the barn for a while. I have put out some rat poison and closed up the barn. I never saw so many fat-looking rats before around the barn." He stroked his beard as he always did when he was puzzled. "They're so big I believe the cats are afraid of them. We must get rid of the rats before harvest time or they will eat up our grain."

John gave Hilda a poke under the table. She gave him a knowing look, then busied herself with her oatmeal. They hadn't meant any harm, and it had been such fun!

After they had finished their chores that morning, John and Hilda sat on the back steps and talked about their pets.

"Poor Samantha and Jennifer," Hilda said with a sigh. "I wonder if they've eaten the poison yet."

"Maybe Ole and Oscar will be too smart to eat the poison," John suggested, hopefully.

"Maybe they'll just smell it and then decide to leave our barn for someplace else."

"I hope so," said Hilda.

For a few minutes they sat in silence; then Hilda had an idea. "I know; let's play with the chickens. Let's marry the roosters to the hens."

John thought it was kind of silly, but he went along when Hilda ran to the chicken pen.

There were six roosters. "What shall we name them?" asked Hilda as the chickens came squawking to meet them.

"It's silly," said John, but he didn't leave.

"The big one can be Mr. Johanson," said Hilda, "and that one Mr. Erickson." She cocked her head to one side for a minute and thought. "I know, Mr. Axsvig, Mr. Thorson, and Mr. Flugstad. Remember which is which. Now we've got to find a wife for each one."

Hilda knew the chickens so well that it wasn't

hard to tell them apart. John finally joined in the game, helping her bring a squawking hen to each squawking rooster.

"Now this is your wife, and don't forget," Hilda told Mr. Johanson, who seemed more interested in looking for grains of corn than in getting married.

It was quite a task to keep the hens with the right roosters. Hilda and John finally left the chickens when Mama called for help with dinner. After dinner, they had to help pick and shell peas for canning. Hilda forgot about the chicken couples until that evening when it was almost bedtime.

"Come on, John," she whispered, "let's go check on the chickens."

Hilda and John ran to the chicken coop. The chickens had already gone to roost.

"John, the roosters aren't with their wives," sighed Hilda. "Let's fix them."

The chickens squawked loudly when the children rearranged them. Mr. Johanson, the big bossy rooster, was especially unhappy about the children's interference with his private life.

The next evening when Hilda and John came to the coop to see that each chicken couple was roosting properly, Mr. Johanson was nowhere to be seen.

"Where could he have gone?" asked John.

"Maybe he's roosting in the trees," suggested Hilda. They ran to look. Mr. Johanson was not in the trees.

"Let's try the pig pen," said John.

They raced to the pig pen, and there on a board, all alone, sat Mr. Johanson with his head snugly tucked under his wing.

John crept stealthily toward him on one side and Hilda on the other. The rooster escaped Hilda's arms, but John caught him. Poor Mr. Johanson let out one forlorn squawk after another as John carried him to the chicken coop.

"Poor thing!" said Hilda. "He probably thinks he's going to the chopping block, and all we want to do is let him be with his very own wife."

Mr. Johanson seemed quite relieved when John plopped him down on the perch in the coop beside Mrs. Johanson. His squawks turned to contented coos.

Satisfied that all was well in the chicken coop, Hilda and John ran back to the house to get ready for bed.

Chapter 11
Run for Your Life

The church Ladies' Missionary Club met once a month at the different homes of the church members. At these meetings the women sewed and knit articles of clothing. Every summer the Ladies' Missionary Club held a picnic in the grove of one of the farms, at which time the articles were sold and the money used to send missionaries to foreign countries.

It was almost time for the missionary picnic, and it was to be held at the Johnsons' place this year. Hilda was so excited. What fun it would be!

"Where will the tables be put if it rains?" she asked Papa one morning when they were talking about the coming event.

"In the granary," answered Papa. "I'm going to put on a new roof, because the old one is beginning to leak. John and I will go to Willmar today to buy the lumber."

"May I go to Willmar, too?" begged Hilda. "It's

such fun to go to the stores and see all the pretty things.''

Papa shook his head. ''No, Hilda, you must stay home and help Mama.''

Hilda turned pleading eyes on Mama.

''The beans are ready to can,'' Mama said, ''and the cucumbers must be picked.''

Hilda began to pout. Why did John get to go when she didn't? Papa acted as if he liked John better than her! She glanced over at John. His happy face made her feel even worse. While she picked beans in the hot sun and snipped them for canning, he would be riding in the wagon to town and seeing all sorts of interesting things when he got there. It wasn't fair!

Papa seemed to know how Hilda felt. He stroked his beard as he frowned thoughtfully. He looked at Mama, but Mama did not give in.

''There is much to do before the picnic,'' she said.

Papa nodded and stood up. ''You're right.'' He turned to Hilda. ''This will be no pleasure trip,

Hilda. John must come along to help me load the lumber. We will come back as soon as possible."

Still Hilda pouted. She didn't smile all day long, even when Mama sent Lois out to the garden with some cool lemonade and cookies for her.

"It isn't fair," she told herself over and over again. "If things were as they used to be before Mama and John came, I'd get to go with Papa. He wouldn't leave me home and make me pick beans all day."

Hilda forgot about the way Mama had cared for her when she had smallpox. She forgot about the kitchen and parlor that Mama had made so pretty and cheery. She forgot about the good things Mama made to eat, the dresses she sewed for her. She forgot, too, about all the fun she had with John.

Hilda helped Mama can twenty-four jars of green beans. They gleamed in the late afternoon sun as they sat proudly on the counter ready to be put away for the winter. But still Hilda sulked.

The next day, while Papa and John were busy making the new roof for the granary, Mr. Peterson appeared. His wife was sick and couldn't cook for their hayers. Would Mrs. Johnson come and help them for the day?

Mama didn't complain, even though she had

planned to make pickles. She simply put things away and got ready to go with Mr. Peterson. She told Hilda how to make dinner and supper for the family. Besides that, she was to take care of Lois and pick the rest of the cucumbers.

Hilda still felt sulky as she peeled potatoes and carrots for dinner. Mama had leftover meat and gravy to warm. There was bread to slice and butter to get from the cellar.

Hilda envied John working on the new roof with Papa. That was more fun than working in the house and garden. After all, Papa belonged to her, not to John.

Papa bragged about the dinner after he had eaten, and patted Hilda's head, but even that didn't make Hilda happy. She looked at the dirty dishes on the table and felt sorry for herself. She hated washing dishes all by herself. Usually Mama washed and she wiped. But now Mama was gone, and she had to wash the kettles and everything.

Lois chattered happily as she tried to help, but her chattering only made Hilda feel cross. She washed so slowly that the water got cold and

greasy. Then it was harder than ever to get the dishes clean.

After finishing the dishes, Hilda took a pail and slowly walked to the garden to pick cucumbers. Lois skipped ahead. It was a sultry day, unusually hot and sticky. Hilda felt more cross than ever.

Papa and John came in late for supper, happy that they had finished the roof. After the supper of warmed-up brown beans, bread, and apple sauce, Papa reached for the Bible to lead in family devotions. A strange rustling sound outside made him look up from the page he was about to read.

"Quick!" he shouted, jumping up. "Run to the cellar!"

Hilda trembled with fear as she watched Papa put out the kerosene light. Papa said "run," but how could she? She was too afraid. Her legs felt like noodles.

Papa grabbed her by one hand and Lois by the other. As they came out of the house, a strong wind nearly blew them over.

"Hurry!" yelled Papa, as they ran to the cellar, John leading the way. Just before they pulled the cellar door shut behind them, Hilda saw a strange sight. A brand-new roof went sailing past her astonished eyes.

Papa saw it, too. Hilda heard him groan. Then he turned and hugged the children, saying over and over again, "Thank God, you are safe! Thank God!"

Hilda trembled for a long while as she heard the torrents of rain come down and the thunder roar outside the cellar. She wanted to pray, but how could she when she had been sulking for two days? God seemed so very far away.

"I wonder how Magda is," Papa kept repeating as he moved nervously about the small cellar. Sometimes he stopped his restless pacing and bowed his head. Hilda knew he was praying. She wished she could pray, but she couldn't.

Finally the storm stopped. Papa led the way out of the cellar. Hilda gasped at the scene that met her eyes. There on the grass behind the house was the new roof shattered into hundreds of pieces!

Papa didn't say much—just led them into the house. A few minutes later they heard voices outside. Then Mama was at the door and in Papa's arms. Mama hugged Lois, John, and Hilda. She said the same thing Papa had, "Thank God, you are safe!"

Mr. Peterson, Papa, Mama, and John went outside to look at the damage caused by the cyclone. Hilda couldn't bear to go out and see the beautiful roof all smashed to pieces. She couldn't bear to think of how unhappy Papa must feel.

Mr. Peterson soon went home, and the others came back into the house.

"We may be able to use a little of the lumber again," Papa said, "but much of it is smashed beyond use." He stroked his beard. "I just don't know if we can afford to buy any more just now. Maybe after I get paid for the hay." He sat down heavily.

"What about the picnic?" asked Hilda. "What if it rains?"

Papa stroked his beard again. "I don't know," he said slowly. "I just don't know."

The Bible lay open on the table in front of him. "Come and sit down for devotions," he said. "I'm going to read something different from what I intended." He began to turn the pages.

Wondering, Hilda sat down across from Papa.

She felt sorry for him and a little bit angry with God for letting the cyclone come to ruin the new roof.

"Here it is," Papa said at last. "I knew I could find it if I looked long enough. Now listen, children. 'Although the fig tree shall not blossom, neither shall fruit be in the vines; the labor of the olive shall fail, and the fields shall yield no meat: the flock shall be cut off from the fold, and there shall be no herd in the stalls; yet I will rejoice in the Lord, I will joy in the God of my salvation.'"

Papa closed the Bible and bowed his head. Hilda waited tensely.

"Heavenly Father, we don't understand why You permit certain things to happen," began Papa, "but we know that You do all things well. We know that all things work together for good to them that love God. So we will thank You no matter what happens, yes, even for the cyclone, even for the ruined roof. And we thank You, too, for keeping us all safe. In Jesus' name, Amen."

"Now let's sing the doxology," said Papa, smiling at them all.

Hilda sang along with the rest, "Praise God from whom all blessings flow," but inside her heart she was saying her own prayer. "Jesus, forgive me for pouting and sulking. Forgive me for being angry with You and everyone else. I want to be like Papa, thankful no matter what happens, thankful and happy even when I have to stay home and pick beans instead of going to town."

The song ended. Everybody smiled as they pushed back their chairs—Hilda, too. It was a relief to feel happy again. Why had she chosen to be miserable? She wouldn't have needed to be if she had thanked God instead of grumbling.

Hilda knew she would never forget the terrifying cyclone. And she would never forget what she had learned from Papa that night about thanking God no matter what happened.

Chapter 12
Missionary Picnic

Because the Johnsons' granary was without a roof, it was decided to have the missionary picnic at Petersons' instead.

At first Hilda felt sad about not having the picnic at their place. But when the Petersons invited them over to help with the preparations, she forgot to feel sad.

Papa and Mr. Peterson made a small platform in their grove of trees with plank seats facing it. That was for the meeting that always came first. Then they built several stands where lemonade, peanuts, candy, cracker jacks, and homemade ice cream would be sold.

Mrs. Peterson and Mama scrubbed their granary, which they would use for the tables in case of rain.

John helped the men, but Hilda and Lois mostly ran between the granary and the grove watching the progress. It was great fun. Hilda could hardly wait until Wednesday, the day of the picnic.

Wednesday dawned clear and bright with not a cloud in the sky. Hilda bounded out of bed as soon as Mama called her.

"Wake up, Lois," she said. "Today's the picnic. Hurry! We've got to help Mama."

Mama must have been up for hours, because three rhubarb pies stood cooling on the counter. She was putting a big pan of baked beans into the oven when Hilda appeared.

"Oh, it smells so good," said Hilda. "Did you stay up all night baking, Mama?"

Mama laughed. "Not quite," she said. "Hurry and wash now so we can get breakfast over with."

After breakfast, Papa counted out ten pennies each for John, Hilda, and Lois. "To spend at the picnic," he explained with a smile.

Hilda hugged Papa and ran to get a clean hanky. She carefully tied her pennies into her hanky and put them in the pocket of her dress. Oh, how rich she felt!

By ten o'clock, everyone was scrubbed, combed, dressed in their best, and ready for the picnic. Mama set the pan of beans wrapped snugly in dish towels at Hilda's feet in the wagon and handed her a pie to hold. Hilda was glad it wasn't too far to Petersons'.

People had already started to gather when the Johnsons arrived. The women were piling the food they had brought onto the long tables set out in the grove. No need to use the granary in this kind of weather. Hilda skipped about the tables with Louise, wondering what was in the dishes and kettles so carefully wrapped and covered.

After all the people had arrived, Pastor Lunde got up on the platform. It was the signal for everyone to sit down on the plank seats. The pastor read from the Bible and prayed. Then he preached a short sermon on missions.

"We are here today not just to enjoy ourselves," he said. "We are here to raise money for missions. We have God's Word to study and a church to attend. We know the way to God through Jesus Christ. Many of us have come to Him for forgiveness and eternal life. But what about the men, women, and children in heathen lands? Some of them have never even heard that there is a Jesus. We must give our money to send missionaries to tell them."

Hilda squirmed on the plank seat. She could feel the ten pennies heavy in her pocket. Papa said the pennies were to spend at the picnic. Why did she feel as if she should give some to help send missionaries?

The pastor kept speaking, but Hilda didn't hear. She was trying to decide what to do about the ten pennies in her hanky.

"We are going to take an offering," said Pastor Lunde at the close of the sermon. "Give as the Lord has given to you. Share with those who have never heard of Jesus."

Hilda pulled the heavy hanky out of her pocket and slowly untied it. She took out a penny and held it tightly in her hand. It was her offering for missions. As she waited for the hat to come by her so she could put in her penny, she thought of the other pennies in her hanky. She was giving one penny to Jesus and keeping nine for herself. It didn't seem quite right.

The hat was coming toward her now. With a pounding heart Hilda took another penny out of her hanky, and when the hat came by her, she dropped two pennies into it. To her surprise, she didn't feel sorry as she thought she might. She felt happy!

After the meeting came the auction. The women had been making things all year to sell. Anton Rude was the auctioneer. He was comical, and Hilda liked him.

"What am I offered?" he said, holding up a man's shirt. "If one of you young fellas wears somethin' fancy as this, you'll get you a wife for sure."

The picnickers paid a good price for the articles, even though most had little money. After all, the money was to be used to send missionaries to foreign countries. They mustn't be stingy.

Soon the dresses, shirts, knitted socks, and quilts had all been sold, and it was time to eat. Hilda was almost too excited to eat. She was glad there was some of Mama's rhubarb pie and Mrs. Peterson's chocolate cake left when she came by to help herself.

The girls took their plates to a grassy spot off by themselves. Just as Hilda was about to sit down, someone bumped her elbow. Her plate flew out of her hand, and the contents landed on the grass. She cried out in dismay. Turning quickly, she saw Pete running off with a smirk on his face.

"That Pete!" she said hotly, with angry tears rushing to her eyes. "He's—he's the meanest boy in the whole world."

Louise tried to comfort her. "Take your plate and get in line again," she said.

"Sure," agreed Marie. "The dogs can eat this stuff on the grass."

Hilda shook her head. "No, I'll eat it myself," she said stubbornly. "I don't want to go back in the line."

The girls helped her scoop up part of the food from the grass. Hilda ate a little, but she didn't enjoy it very much. She was so angry with Pete! He had to spoil everything—even the picnic.

"Let's go to the stands," suggested Louise. "I want a cracker jack and some ice cream."

The girls returned their plates to the table and raced to the stands, where the men were cranking freezers to make ice cream.

"Hold on," shouted Mr. Peterson, who was cranking with all his might. "It'll be a few minutes before it's ready."

"We'll wait," said Louise.

Hilda pulled her hanky out of her pocket and carefully took out three pennies. That's how much an ice-cream cone cost.

Others crowded around the stand. John and

Nels came, and some of the other boys. Hilda stiffened when she saw Pete milling around with the rest. He pushed his way up to the front where the girls were waiting.

"You can't crowd into the line," said Louise crossly.

"Who says I can't?" he retorted.

Hilda bit her lip to keep from saying something nasty. Why did Pete have to come to the picnic, anyway? The picnic would be perfect if it weren't for him.

At last the ice cream was ready. As Hilda licked the cold, sweet, creamy goodness, she thought she had never tasted anything so delicious in her life. While she ate her ice cream, she didn't even think about Pete and his pranks.

"Let's get a cracker jack," said Louise, when they had finished their ice cream. "Or would you rather have candy?"

"Both," answered Hilda with a laugh. "If I have enough pennies left," she added. She reached for the knotted hanky in her pocket. Suddenly she felt sick. It wasn't there!

"What's wrong?" asked Louise, noticing Hilda's stricken face.

"My money—it's gone!" gasped Hilda.

"Are you sure? Look in both pockets."

"I did. It isn't here."

"Let's go back to the ice-cream stand. Maybe you dropped it after you paid for your ice cream."

The girls hurried over to the stand, where a group of people were waiting in line for ice cream. Mr. Peterson was filling cones.

Hilda felt like crying. How could she look for her lost money when so many people were milling around by the stand? She couldn't tell them all to get out of the way so she could look.

"Come on, Louise," she said, grabbing her friend's hand. "It's no use."

Tears rushed to Hilda's eyes so she couldn't see well. Angrily, she brushed them away. She wouldn't let all these people see her cry for anything. Suddenly, she spied John busily devouring the contents of a cracker-jack box.

"Come on, Louise," she said. "I'm going to tell John."

John seemed sorry that Hilda had lost her

money. "I'll go look," he said. "I'm not afraid to ask the people to move."

Hilda watched anxiously as John searched all around the ice-cream stand. He even asked Mr. Peterson if someone had turned in a hanky with five pennies in it. Nobody had.

John shook his head as he joined the girls. "It's not anywhere around," he said. "You know what I think? Somebody stole it. Bet it was Pete."

Hilda remembered that Pete had been crowding to the front when she opened her hanky to get out the pennies for the ice cream. "Would he do such a terrible thing as steal my pennies?" she asked.

"Pete would do *anything*," piped up Louise. "He's still mad about the way you jumped on him when he was beating up John."

John scowled and turned away. He didn't like to be reminded of that. Nels came running towards him. "C'mon, John," he said, "they're going to have races. Let's be partners in the three-legged one."

"All right," said John. He started to go with Nels, then stopped. "Wait a minute," he said. Walking back to where Hilda and Louise still stood in mournful silence, he put his hand in his pocket.

"Here," he said, handing Hilda three pennies. "You can buy a cracker jack."

Hilda was too surprised to answer. John sharing his precious pennies with her? She could hardly believe it. She watched him run off with Nels.

"What are we waiting for?" asked Louise. "Let's go get a cracker jack, and we can eat it while we watch the races."

Hilda shook her head. "Not me," she said. "I'm going to get another ice-cream cone."

The girls ran joyfully to the stand. Hilda was so happy, she felt like flying. It wasn't only because she could have some more delicious ice cream, but it was also because she had such a nice brother.

When she got home, she was going to climb her maple tree and say a special thank you to God!

Chapter 13
Tramps and Mischief

It was hot, so hot that nobody felt like doing anything. Of course, Papa and Mama worked even when it was hot, but they didn't require the children to do much.

Hilda helped Mama carry the dinner and the dishes outside. It was too hot to eat in the kitchen, where the cookstove had been burning. Under the elm tree in the yard they could at least get a little breeze.

"Mama and I are going to town right after dinner," announced Papa, as they were eating their stew under the elm tree.

"Can we go, too?" asked John, Hilda, and Lois in unison.

Papa shook his head. "Not this time. I want you to take the cows out to the hay fields this afternoon. The pasture is getting so bare, but they should find something to eat where we have cut the hay."

Hilda smiled at Lois. They liked herding the cows. It was a time to tell make-believe stories and play pretend games.

"Do the dishes first," said Mama. "We should be home in time for me to make supper."

A few minutes later, the children watched Mama

and Papa drive off in the wagon. They knew they should start the dishes, but it was so pleasant just to lie in the shade! Hilda liked to look at the clear blue sky through the shimmering green leaves that moved lazily in the breeze.

Suddenly, John's voice startled Hilda. "Hey, somebody's coming. It looks like a tramp!"

Hilda sat up quickly and looked. Her heart pounded with fear. Sure enough, a tramp was coming up the driveway right towards the house.

"Oh, John," she cried in dismay, "what shall we do?"

"Sshh," warned John. "Don't let on you're scared." He turned to Lois. "Run into the house and stay there," he said sternly. Lois did as she was told.

The Johnson house wasn't too far from the railroad tracks, so tramps sometimes stopped to

ask for food. Mama always gave them something. But today Mama wasn't there, and neither was Papa! Some tramps were harmless, men without jobs who were going from one place to another looking for work. Others were rascals and thieves. Not knowing which were which, people looked upon them all with suspicion.

"Howdy!" said the tramp, when he reached the shade of the elm tree.

"Hello," answered John. All Hilda could do was stare.

The man looked younger than Papa. He threw his black hat on the ground and sat down beside it. He had red hair and a reddish-brown beard. His shirt wasn't buttoned, and his trousers were raggedy. Sweat rolled down his face and chest.

"How about some grub?" he asked, after he had rested a minute.

John turned to Hilda. "Go ask Mama," he said.

Hilda stared at John. Ask Mama? Mama wasn't home. How could she ask her?

John frowned at her. "But don't disturb Papa," he continued. "He likes his afternoon rest."

Hilda still stared.

"Hurry," said John. "This man is hungry."

Suddenly Hilda understood. It was like a game, one of their pretend ones, only this one was somehow terribly real. She ran into the kitchen.

"Mama!" she called, loudly enough for the

tramp outside to hear. She put her hand over Lois's mouth. "Don't say a word," she whispered in her little sister's ear. "Stay right here!"

In a moment, Hilda ran out of the house carrying a plate, knife, fork, and cup. "We may give him what is left," she said.

Hilda scraped the leftover stew onto the plate and put it on the table. She offered the tramp bread and butter. John filled his cup with water from the pump in the yard.

The tramp ate as though he hadn't seen food for a long time. Hilda felt sorry for him. She wouldn't like to be a tramp, going from place to place, sleeping wherever he could, begging for food.

After he had eaten, the man stretched out in the shade and went to sleep. Hilda looked questioningly at John. His mouth formed the words: "You do the dishes; I'll watch him."

Hilda thought John was very brave. She carried the dishes into the house and began to wash them. Lois helped dry. She was full of questions about the tramp. Hilda didn't dare tell her too much. Lois was the world's worst secret-keeper, and the tramp must not find out that they were alone.

Hilda ran from the dishpan to the window several times to see if the man was still sleeping. The last time she looked, she saw the man stand up, brush off his ragged trousers, and saunter away in the direction of the railroad tracks. She breathed a huge sigh of relief.

John came into the house. Hilda knew that he, too, was relieved that the tramp was gone, but he wouldn't admit it. They laughed as they remembered how they had fooled him.

"I didn't lie," declared John stoutly. "I just told you to ask Mama and not to wake Papa. I didn't say they were in the house."

They laughed again. Hilda thought John quite clever to outsmart the tramp. She wrung out the dishcloth and threw the water out the back door. Suddenly, she thought of the cows.

"What about the cows, John?" she asked. "Papa told us to take them to the hayfields."

John frowned thoughtfully. Hilda could tell that he was feeling very much like a man after doing so well with the tramp. "Somebody should stay here, in case he comes back," he said.

"Or another one!" exclaimed Hilda. "Sometimes they steal things when nobody's home."

"Do you want to stay?" asked John.

Hilda shivered in spite of the heat. "Oh, no! Lois and I will herd the cows. It would be safer in the hayfields than here at home."

"Maybe so," agreed John. "Tramps usually go to houses, where they can get food. You would be safer in the hayfields, all right."

Hilda and Lois ran to take the cows from the pasture to the hayfields. The three cows were glad to go to a new eating place and followed the girls willingly.

Hilda and Lois found a shady spot by some bushes and sat down to rest while the cows grazed.

"Tell me a story," begged Lois.

Hilda chewed on a piece of hay while she thought of a story for Lois. Finally, she decided to make up one. It was a story about tramps.

Lois shivered when it was over. "Is it true?" she whispered.

"Well, a little bit," answered Hilda, thinking of her recent encounter with the tramp. "But not much," she added. She mustn't scare Lois.

They were tired of sitting by now. "Let's make a wigwam out of grass," suggested Hilda.

The girls found a place where the wild grasses were tall and coarse. Taking a piece of grass for a string, they tied a clump of grass together at the top. Then they pulled out the grass inside to make a room. It was a perfect wigwam.

"You find some flat stones for furniture," said Hilda to Lois, "and I'll make some Indian people out of grass."

Lois was so busy looking for stones and Hilda so intent on twisting grass into pretend people that they forgot all about the cows. Suddenly, Hilda jumped up.

"Lois!" she cried. "The cows! Where are they?"

"I don't know," answered Lois.

"Come on, we've got to find them!"

The girls started across the hayfield. It was hard to walk across the stubble, but they didn't think

of that, so intent were they on finding the missing
cows.

"I think I see them," cried Lois. "See,
something black over there."

Hilda looked where Lois pointed. Sure enough,
there was something black moving towards them.
But it wasn't a cow.

"Lois," she gasped, "that's not a cow. That's
a tramp!"

Lois started to cry. Hilda felt like crying, too,
but she couldn't. She had to think of what to do.

Tramps were looking for food and things to
steal. Why would one come to a hayfield? What
did he want?

"Quick, Lois," she said, "lie flat on the ground.
Maybe he won't see us."

Just then the figure in black waved at them.

"Oh," gasped Hilda,"he *does* see us. What will
we do?"

Lois cried and clung to Hilda. Hilda just stared
at the frightening figure moving towards them.
She wanted to run, but somehow her legs
wouldn't work.

Suddenly, the tramp turned a somersault.
Getting to his feet, he waved his arms wildly and
yelled, all the while coming closer.

"It's not only a tramp," sobbed Hilda, "it's
a *crazy* tramp." She was too frightened to
remember she shouldn't say things to scare Lois.

'Come on, Lois, run!" she commanded, grabbing her sister's hand and starting off across the hayfield. The ground was uneven and the stubble hard to run on. Lois fell. As Hilda stopped to help her up, she heard laughing behind her. She looked around.

There stood John, dressed up in some raggedy trousers and an old black hat of Papa's. He laughed so hard, he finally had to roll on the ground.

Hilda felt so relieved that the tramp was John, she forgot to be angry with him for scaring them. That is, she forgot until she heard Lois wail beside her, "I want Mama! I want Papa!"

"See what you've done!" scolded Hilda, trying to soothe Lois.

"Aw, I didn't mean anything," said John, still laughing. "Mama and Papa came home, and I was telling them about the tramp. I put on this old hat of Papa's to show them what he looked like. Then I found these ragged barn pants. When they told me to fetch you and Lois and the cows home, I thought it would be fun to—"

"Scare us half to death," finished Hilda. She wasn't really as angry as she sounded. She couldn't forget the three pennies John had given her at the missionary picnic the other day.

Suddenly, Hilda remembered the cows. "John,

the cows have wandered away! Will you help us find them?''

''I thought you came out here to watch them,'' John teased, his brown eyes dancing.

''We made a wigwam and forgot to watch,'' Lois piped up, still sniffing.

''Don't worry,'' said John. ''I saw them when I came. They're over in that direction. Come on, before they decide to move on.''

They walked on in silence for a few minutes. Then Hilda said, ''Let's hold Lois's hands and run. We can get there faster.'' They laughed as they fairly flew across the field to where the cows were munching contentedly and not lost at all.

Chapter 14
Secret in the Cupboard

Hilda waited and waited for a letter from Valerie, but it never came. She was afraid she had lost her chance to share her wonderful secret with her friend.

"I wonder if there's anyone else I should share it with," she said to herself one rainy September morning. "All my other friends already know about Jesus. They go to church and Sunday school just as I do."

All except Pete. He didn't. Pete's parents had both died several years before, and Pete lived with his two uncles. His uncles didn't come to church, either, except at Christmas and Easter. Then Pete came, too.

Hilda and John were shelling dried beans by the kitchen table. Papa had taken Mama over to Mrs. Peterson's to make green tomato relish. He was going to help Mr. Peterson fix his plow. At the last minute, Mama said that Lois might come along.

Hilda didn't really mind staying home. She and John could think of something fun to do when they finished shelling the beans.

"Don't worry about tramps," Papa had said before he left. "They wouldn't come around in rainy weather like this. Besides, they're like the birds— when it starts to get cold, they go south."

While they shelled beans, Hilda asked John about Pete. "Do you really think he stole my money at the picnic?" she asked.

John shrugged. "How could I know? People say he's stolen things before. Once they caught him down at the general store with three peppermint sticks in his pocket that he hadn't paid for."

Hilda shook her head unbelievingly. "And to think that he comes to our school!"

"He's not there half the time. Guess his uncles keep him pretty busy helping with the feed business." John emptied his small pan of shelled beans into the big one on the table.

"Too bad Pete doesn't come to church so he could learn about Jesus. Then maybe he wouldn't do so many bad things."

"He won't come," said John, "except at Christmas, when we get candy and apples."

Hilda frowned. "Then maybe we'll have to tell him about Jesus ourselves."

"Humph!" snorted John. Hilda could tell he didn't think much of her idea.

"Let's play a game," said Hilda. "I see something blue, white, and red."

John looked all over the kitchen before he noticed it was Hilda's apron.

"I see something brown, yellow, and orange," said John.

"The rug by the door!" shouted Hilda.

After a while they grew tired of their guessing games. "Let's play something else," suggested John. "How about 'Hide the Thimble'?"

"We can't do that while we shell beans," protested Hilda.

"Sure we can. You shell while I hide it, and I'll shell while you hide it." John jumped up. "I'll be first," he said, running to get Mama's thimble out of her sewing basket.

Hilda turned her chair so she couldn't see into the parlor. Soon John came back, his eyes sparkling.

"Ready," he said.

Hilda went into the parlor, looking carefully in every place she thought a thimble might be hiding.

"You're cold," John said. "You're really cold." That meant she wasn't anywhere near the thimble. Where could it be? She raised her eyes to the ceiling. Could John have stuck it up there someplace?

John shook his head. "Cold as ice," he said.

Hilda moved toward the kitchen. "You're a tiny bit warmer, but still cold," John said.

Hilda moved toward Mama and Papa's bedroom.

"You're getting warmer," said John.

"You didn't hide it in their bedroom, did you?" asked Hilda in shocked tones. "We're not allowed to play in there."

John shrugged. "Just hiding a thimble isn't playing."

Hilda hesitated at the door.

"Aw, come on, Hilda," begged John, "just this time. I won't hide it in there my next turn."

"All right," agreed Hilda. It was kind of fun to look around in Mama and Papa's bedroom. Papa had built a little cupboard on one side of the wall. Had John hidden the thimble in there? Hilda pulled open the door.

"Cold! Cold!" shouted John.

Hilda didn't answer. She stared into the cupboard, then turned to John with wide eyes.

"John," she whispered, "look what's in here!" She lifted up a tiny baby nightgown and a tiny shirt.

John's eyes opened wide. He came closer to look.

Hilda was so excited her fingers trembled. "Look, tiny booties!" She held them up for John to see. "And a pile of flannel blankets! Oh, John," she squealed, "do you suppose we're going to get a baby?"

John shook his head. "I don't know," he said. "Maybe."

Hilda folded the tiny baby clothes and put them back just as she had found them. She was so excited she couldn't speak.

"If we do get a baby, I hope it'll be a boy," John said.

"Oh, I hope it's a girl!" exclaimed Hilda, shutting the cupboard carefully.

"We've already got two girls," answered John. "We need another boy."

Hilda thought about that as they went out of the bedroom. Yes, she had to admit, a little brother would be nice for John. She had Lois, even though she wasn't very little any more. Baby boys were almost as cute as baby girls.

"I guess you're right," she said with a sigh. "It's all right if it's a boy."

With that decided, the two sat down by the beans again and started to shell. For a few minutes neither of them spoke. Each knew what the other was thinking about—the new baby.

Finally, Hilda looked up from the beans in her lap. "John," she said, "about the baby, I don't think we can decide. Whether it's a boy or girl, I mean. God decides, doesn't He?"

"Yah," agreed John.

"And He'll know which is best for our family, a girl or a boy."

"I guess so."

All that could be heard in the kitchen was the cracking of the dried bean pods and the beans dropping into the pans. Finally, John looked up from his work and grinned.

"Hey, you didn't find the thimble," he said.

"I don't care," said Hilda. "You go get it and put it back in Mama's sewing basket. We'd better not play in her room any more. We might find another secret."

John hurried off to bring the thimble. Hilda stopped shelling beans for a minute and looked out the window with a faraway look in her eyes. One secret was enough for today, especially when it was such an exciting one.

Chapter 15
Birthday Surprise

School started again in October, after the threshing was over. Hilda could hardly wait to see her teacher again and all her friends. She could hardly wait to see if there were new books to read and new pictures hung on the walls.

John acted as if he didn't want to go back to school, but Hilda was sure he was only pretending. School was fun.

Nels had grown so much during the summer that he was as tall as Pete, and his shoulders were broader. Pete didn't dare pick fights with the younger boys when Nels was around. Instead, he began to torment the girls. He yanked their braids, hid their lunches, and came up behind them and yelled so they got scared and dropped their books. Pete was a real pest at school. Nobody liked him.

Hilda's birthday was October 12. It was a special day at school as well as at home, because Miss Dahlen kept track of everyone's birthday. She always gave the birthday child a brightly colored card with a wise saying on it. Everybody joined in singing "Happy Birthday" after the morning prayer, and when any errands needed to be run, Miss Dahlen chose the birthday child.

Hilda skipped into the schoolhouse on the morning of her birthday feeling happy and special. Miss Dahlen smiled at her.

"Good morning, Hilda," she said, "and happy birthday." She held out a brightly colored card.

"Oh, thank you, Miss Dahlen!" exclaimed Hilda as she took the pretty card. She studied it on the way to her desk. On the card was a baby angel with pink roses twined about her. At the bottom were written the words: "Do unto others as you would have others do unto you."

With a happy sigh, Hilda tucked the card into her desk. As she did so, she felt something bulky in there. She leaned over and peeked in. There was a package wrapped in brown paper in her desk. Somebody had given her a birthday present. Who could it be?

Hilda's fingers trembled with excitement as she slid the package out of the desk onto her lap. She didn't want anyone to see her open it, especially since she didn't know who it was from. Taking off the string, she carefully pulled back the paper. What she saw made her jump and almost scream. It was a cow's tail!

Hilda shoved the package back into her desk without a word, her eyes brimming with angry tears. She knew who had played the joke on her. It couldn't be anybody else but Pete. Well, she'd show him. She'd think of something mean to do in return.

Hilda heard loud snickering in the back of the room. No doubt Pete had been watching her. Well, she wouldn't even look around. Someday he'd be sorry for the way he was acting.

Miss Dahlen opened the school day with Bible reading and prayer. "Now let's sing 'Happy Birthday' to Hilda," she said. "Hilda is nine years old today."

Hilda looked down while they sang for her. She liked the song, and she liked the beautiful card her teacher had given her. But the cow's tail in her desk took some of the pleasure out of her day and made her feel cross.

Miss Dahlen had jobs for Hilda to do during recess and noon hour, important jobs like helping her put pictures on the wall and grade papers. In the afternoon, Miss Dahlen let her choose a friend to help her go to the pump outdoors to fill the water pail for the school children. It would have been a perfect day had it not been for the cow's tail.

Hilda told John about it on the way home from school. "I'm sure it was Pete," she said. "Nobody

else would be so mean. I wish I could pay him
back. It would serve him right.''

"Maybe you can give him something at the
Christmas program that would make him mad.''

"Like what?'' asked Hilda. "A dead mouse or
something?''

"Naw,'' answered John. "Boys don't mind
things like that. Why don't you give him
something for a girl, like a doll. He'd really hate
that.''

"If I had a doll I wouldn't give it away,''
retorted Hilda. "I'd keep it.''

"We'll think of something,'' said John, as they
turned into the lane that led to their house.

The children found Mama busy with a special
birthday supper for Hilda, and Hilda didn't even
have to set the table. After she had changed her
clothes, she ran out to her maple tree. It was
best that she was out of the way when the family
was fixing surprises for her. Besides, Hilda wanted
to talk to God about the happenings of the day.

When Hilda climbed the tree, she told God about the pretty card, the birthday song, and about helping Miss Dahlen at school. She told Him about the cow's tail, too, but somehow she couldn't ask God to help her get even with Pete. She just couldn't. Feeling a little bewildered, she slid down from the tree and skipped into the house.

The birthday supper was such fun! Mama had made meatballs and gravy, Hilda's favorite, and biscuits. For dessert there was a cake with sugar icing and nine candles. And there was a present to make Hilda's happiness complete. Mama had tatted pink lace around a white hanky, and Papa had tied up a dime in it. Hilda squeezed them both and then ran to get her pretty card to show Papa.

After admiring the baby angel and roses, Papa read the words at the bottom of the card, "Do unto others as you would have others do unto you." The words reminded Hilda of the cow's tail.

"Pete sure doesn't do what that says," she reflected darkly. And then she told her family about the cow's tail in her desk.

"I know it was Pete, because nobody else would be so mean. Besides, I heard him laugh after I opened it. I wish I could pay him back somehow." For some reason Hilda felt a little guilty as she said the words, but she said them anyway.

"I know how you can pay him back," answered Papa quickly.

Hilda looked at Papa in surprise. She hadn't expected any help from Papa in this kind of project.

"Heap coals of fire on his head," said Papa, stroking his beard.

Hilda stared at Papa. What could he mean? He couldn't be serious.

Papa's eyes were twinkling, but he was serious.

"Papa doesn't mean real coals," explained Mama. "Jesus said that if your enemy is hungry, you should feed him, and if he's thirsty, you should give him a drink, and that way you'll be heaping coals of fire on his head."

"Not real coals then?" asked John, looking a little disappointed.

Papa shook his head. "It means that when you're good to somebody who is mean to you,

you make him uncomfortable about the way he has treated you. Maybe he'll even be sorry.''

''Not Pete,'' said Hilda, shaking her head.

Papa asked Lois to bring the Bible. ''Listen to Jesus' words,'' he said. '''But I say unto you, Love your enemies, bless them that curse you, do good to them that hate you, and pray for them who despitefully use you, and persecute you.'''

Hilda smoothed her dress over her knees and thought hard. Love Pete? How could she?

''Pete doesn't have much of a home,'' said Mama. ''I wonder if he even gets decent food half the time, with no woman around to cook.''

Papa shook his head. ''And those uncles of his—the way they guzzle the bottle!''

''I've never thought about that before,'' said Hilda slowly, twirling the end of her braid. She remembered how it was before Mama came, but at least she had Papa, and he didn't drink.

''Let's do as Jesus says,'' went on Papa. ''Let's pray for Pete.''

Hilda closed her eyes and bowed her head. Papa usually said a special birthday prayer for her on her birthday, but tonight he was praying for Pete. Hilda didn't mind. She decided that from now on she would pray for Pete, too, and she would ask Jesus to help her like him even if he was mean.

John cleared the table, Mama washed the dishes, and Lois wiped. Hilda sat in the rocking chair reading her library book and enjoying the last minutes of her special day.

Hilda sighed when it was time to go upstairs to bed. It had been such a lovely day that she didn't want it to end. Taking her colored card and the pretty hanky with the shiny dime, she slowly climbed the stairs. How rich she felt! The cow's tail didn't even matter any more.

Snug under the covers beside Lois a few minutes later, Hilda thought about the words on the card her teacher had given her: "Do unto others as you would have others do unto you."

She couldn't be mean back to Pete if she was going to obey those words. But what could she do? Suddenly, Hilda had an idea. She would give Pete a *nice* Christmas present under the Christmas tree at the Christmas program. He would be surprised, and he would be glad.

Now that she had decided, Hilda could hardly wait until morning so she could tell John. Hilda felt happier than she had all day.

Chapter 16
The Blizzard and a Surprise

The day started out pleasant enough. It hadn't been terribly cold as Hilda and John had crunched to school through the snow. Right after recess, though, the wind changed to the northwest and it began to snow. The wind began to blow harder. The schoolhouse creaked and groaned as snow and wind battered it angrily.

Hilda shivered as she heard the wind howling and the fine icy snow striking the sides of the building. Miss Dahlen went to the window and looked out anxiously. Hilda wondered why she bothered. She could see nothing, anyway, except swirling snow.

All the children, except for the very small ones, knew enough to be afraid of Minnesota blizzards. Hilda could tell as she looked around that everyone else was as scared as she was. How could they ever walk home in this weather? Would they have to stay in the schoolhouse all night? But what would they eat? Would there be enough wood to burn to keep them warm?

Hilda jumped when she heard the loud stomping in the school's entryway. The next moment, she felt happy all over. There were Papa, Mr. Larsen, and some of the other men, who had come to take the children home.

Mama had sent flatirons wrapped in cloths to keep their feet warm on the sled. She had sent plenty of blankets, too. Hilda and John huddled under the blankets; they felt sorry for Papa driving the horses with little or no shelter from the storm. It seemed like forever before the sled jerked to a stop.

Hilda heaved a sigh of relief when she saw that they had arrived home safely. Papa carried her, wrapped in blankets, into the house; and John stumbled after them.

Papa looked like a snowman. His cap was covered with snow. His eyebrows and beard were white and crusty. For a few minutes, he warmed himself by the stove while Mama tried to brush off the snow.

"This one is a humdinger!" exclaimed Papa. "I must get the horses into the barn. Poor things—they'll be frozen stiff."

When Papa stepped out of the door, the icy wind blew in, making the whole kitchen cold. Hilda crept closer to the stove.

Mama walked back and forth with an anxious look on her face. "I'm afraid for Papa," she said. "We should have given him a rope."

"I'll take him one," offered John.

Mama shook her head. "Then what if you get lost?"

"I won't. Tie it around my waist. I'll find the barn."

There was a rope in the lean-to shed behind the kitchen. The wind was blowing so strongly it nearly blew Mama over when she went out to help John find it. She tied one end of the rope around John's waist and the other to a beam of the lean-to.

"I hate to send you out in this storm," she said.

Hilda watched from the window, but she could not see John. All she could see was dazzling white snow whirling madly about, making her feel like a prisoner in her own home. She turned and walked to the stove. The wind was forcing its icy breath through every crack in the house, but at least it was a little warm by the stove.

Mama began to churn butter with all her might. It seemed to Hilda, who was watching her, that she was trying to compete with the howling blizzard outside. Suddenly, Mama stopped churning. Her face turned pale as she put her hand on her stomach.

"Come, Hilda," she said, "churn for me. I— I—" She sank into the rocking chair by the stove.

Hilda watched her anxiously as she pushed the churn handle up and down, up and down. When it would no longer move easily, she knew the cream had turned to butter. "I think it's done, Mama," she said.

Mama stood up wearily. "Thank you, Hilda," she said. "I'll do the rest."

"I'll help you," offered Hilda. "What do you need—salt?"

Mama nodded. "And cold water to rinse it off. Bring the brown bowl, too. I'll put it in that."

Soon the butter was washed, salted, and ready for the table. Mama sat down heavily in the rocking chair again. Hilda peered out of the

window once more, but it was no use. She couldn't see a thing but swirling snow.

When Hilda heard feet stomping in the lean-to, she ran to open the door. Papa and John were brushing off as much snow as possible before they came in by the fire. Hilda was so glad to see them!

"It's a good thing you sent John," said Papa when he was warmed up enough to speak. "I'm afraid I wouldn't have found the house otherwise."

Hilda shivered at the thought. Lois ran to Mama and crawled up in her lap as if she were afraid the cruel blizzard would somehow get her.

"The rope was a good idea," said Papa. "I fastened it to the barn. Now I'll be able to get out to do the chores no matter how long this blizzard lasts."

"Will it last a long time?" asked Hilda, anxiously.

Papa shook his head. "Who knows? Sometimes these blizzards last several days."

"I have hot bean soup for you," said Mama. "That'll help to warm you up."

It took Hilda a long time to get warm in bed that night, even though Lois slept beside her and they had warm flatirons for their feet. She hoped the blizzard wouldn't last very long. Christmas would soon be here, and the children had to practice for the school program as well as for the one at church.

And what about the new baby? This was no kind of weather for her. Or was there going to be a new baby? Mama hadn't said anything. Maybe the baby clothes were for some other family. Hilda wished she knew, but she didn't dare ask.

She snuggled down into the covers and was lulled to sleep at last by the howling wind.

Hilda woke up the next morning with sunshine streaming in the window. It made her feel cheerful. Jumping out of bed, she ran down the icy cold stairway to the kitchen below. Mama was punching down the bread. She looked tired.

"Good morning, Mama," Hilda said. "May I dress by the stove?"

Mama nodded. "It's not very warm even by the stove today," she said.

"Why didn't you wake me?" asked Hilda.

"There'll be no school today with all these snow drifts. I thought you might as well stay in bed where it was warm."

"Where's John?" asked Hilda, as she pulled her warm, woolen dress over her long, woolen underwear and fastened a knitted shawl over her shoulders.

"He went with Papa to haul some of the hay by the slough. Papa wants to be sure he has plenty for the livestock before another blizzard comes."

Hilda started to eat the hot oatmeal Mama dished up for her. It felt good to have something warm in her stomach. She shivered in spite of her warm clothes. The stove wasn't doing a very good job of heating the kitchen today. Hilda wandered into the parlor. The heating stove didn't seem to be giving off as much heat as usual, either.

"Call Lois, and give her some oatmeal," said Mama. "Then come and wash the dishes. The dishwater will warm you up." Mama went into the parlor and lay down on the sofa.

Hilda followed her. "Don't you feel well, Mama?" she asked.

Mama shook her head. "No, Hilda, I don't. When Papa comes back I will ask him to get the doctor. He should be back soon."

Hilda called Lois and dished up her oatmeal. Then she washed the dishes. She was thinking so hard about Mama that she wiped the dishes herself instead of asking Lois to help.

Suddenly, she heard a groan from the parlor. Still holding the dish towel and bowl she was drying, Hilda ran to Mama's side. Mama's white face scared her.

"What is it, Mama," she cried, "are you so very sick?"

Mama closed her eyes. "Yes, Hilda," she said weakly. "Could you hitch one of the horses to the sled and go to Petersons' for help? It's too late to get the doctor, but if Mrs. Peterson could come—" Her voice trailed off.

Hilda leaned over and kissed Mama's pale cheek. "I'll get Mrs. Peterson. Don't worry, Mama."

Hilda took Mama's big shawl to put over her coat and a blanket to put over her lap. It would be cold riding on the sled on a day like this.

"Goodbye, Lois," she said to her little sister. "You take care of Mama, and I'll be right back."

An icy blast of wind hit Hilda's face when she stepped out of the lean-to. She gasped when she saw the piles of snow all around. Papa had shoveled a path to the barn, so Hilda had no trouble reaching it.

With fingers already cold in spite of her woolen mittens, Hilda opened the barn door. There stood the cows, Daisy, Lady, and Dolly, patiently munching hay, but the horses were not there. Papa and John had taken them to haul the hay, of course, and the sled, too. Mama must be very sick to have forgotten.

For a moment, Hilda stood undecided as to what to do. Should she go back to the house and tell Mama she couldn't get Mrs. Peterson after all? But how could she do that when Mama was so sick and needed help?

"I'll have to walk," said Hilda. "It isn't too terribly far. There is no other way." Stepping out of the barn and pulling the door shut firmly behind herself, she ran to the house and across the field to the road. The icy wind slapped her face, chilling her to the bone.

The wind had blown the snow into drifts of all shapes and sizes. Sometimes Hilda stepped into places so deep she could hardly scramble out. Sometimes the snow was firm where the wind had blown the new snow away, but more often Hilda sank down to her knees.

Hilda's nose and eyes began to run. The icy wind made her gasp for breath. It became harder to press through the soft snow. She stumbled and fell when her feet refused to move as fast as the rest of her. On and on she went, falling again and again, and then picking herself up. Once when she fell she didn't get up right away. The snow didn't feel as cold as the wind. She just lay there, thinking that she couldn't make it to Petersons', anyway, or even back home again.

Suddenly, Hilda understood what was happening to her. That was how people froze to death. She couldn't lie in the snow. She couldn't give up. She had to keep moving. But how could she? It was so cold, and her feet didn't want to obey her any more!

Hilda forced herself to get up. She tried to jump up and down to bring her feet back to life. That helped a little, and she pressed on. On and on and on she plodded, head bent before the wind. It was like a bad, bad dream that never ended.

Finally, Hilda stopped and looked around her. Terror struck her. Where was she? She could see no houses or barns and no roads. All she could see was snow, snow, and more snow.

"Jesus," she cried, with tears rolling down her

cheeks. "I'm lost. I'm lost in the snow. Please help me."

Hilda had lived in Minnesota long enough to know she had to keep moving to survive. Even if it seemed impossible, she had to keep going, on and on and on until she reached shelter.

But what if she wasn't even on the road? What if she was going in the wrong direction altogether?

"Jesus, help me," she sobbed as she plodded ahead. She couldn't even feel her hands and feet anymore. How much longer could she keep moving?

The wind began to blow more fiercely. Snow began to swirl before Hilda's eyes and hit her in the face.

"Another blizzard!" she gasped. But somehow she was too numb and too tired to care. If she fell again, she wouldn't bother to get up.

Hilda heard something through her numbness. Was it voices? Or was she dreaming?

The sounds came closer. Mustering all her strength, she waved her arms and screamed. In

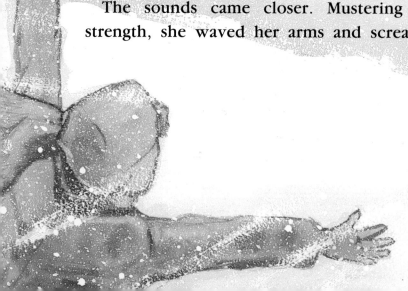

a moment, Papa was beside her, gathering her
up in his strong arms.

"My poor little girl," he said over and over
again. "Thank God we found you."

Papa lifted Hilda onto the sled and covered her
with blankets. John was there, too, and Mr.
Peterson.

"Home, Prince. Home, Taffy!" ordered Papa.
He gave the reins to Mr. Peterson so he could
hold Hilda. The blizzard was getting worse, but
the horses seemed to know their way home. John
and Mr. Peterson put the horses in the barn while
Papa carried Hilda into the house and set her
down in the rocking chair by the stove. Lois ran
to her with a cry of joy. The warmth of the
stove felt both wonderful and terrible to Hilda,
terrible because it made her half-frozen feet and
hands hurt so much.

"It's good if they hurt," said Papa, rubbing
them gently. "That means they are not frozen
too badly. They'll soon stop hurting, and you'll
be as good as new again."

Suddenly, Hilda remembered something. "Mrs. Peterson!" she gasped. "I was supposed to get Mrs. Peterson for Mama."

"She's in there," said Lois, pointing to the bedroom with her chin, "with Mama."

"She came on their sled," explained Papa, "and we went to look for you."

Papa left Hilda to go into the bedroom. Hilda leaned back in the rocking chair. It felt so good to rest! Mrs. Peterson and Papa were with Mama. Everything would be all right.

Mr. Peterson and John came in from putting the horses in the barn and warmed themselves by the fire. Suddenly, Hilda heard something strange. It sounded like a kitten crying.

The bedroom door opened, and Papa came into the kitchen carrying a small bundle wrapped in soft blankets. "Meet your baby brother," he said.

Hilda ran to look. She was so happy, she thought her heart would burst!

Chapter 17
Christmas

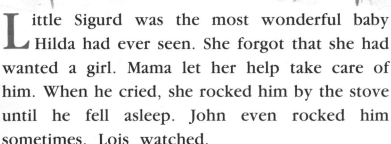

L ittle Sigurd was the most wonderful baby Hilda had ever seen. She forgot that she had wanted a girl. Mama let her help take care of him. When he cried, she rocked him by the stove until he fell asleep. John even rocked him sometimes. Lois watched.

A few days before Christmas, Papa took the sled to town. Hilda didn't even mind that she couldn't go along. It was more fun to stay home and care for Sigurd than to go to town. She gave John her birthday dime to buy something for Pete. She could hardly wait until they came home to show her what they had bought.

It was almost dark when John burst into the house. He was as excited as Hilda about the shiny jackknife he had bought for Pete with Hilda's dime.

Hilda wrapped it up in some white paper Mama found for her and tied one of her wornout hair ribbons around it. ''To Pete from John and Hilda,''

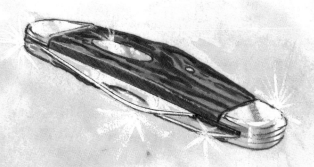

she wrote on the white paper. "What would Pete think of it?" she wondered. She hoped he would know that she and John liked him and wanted to be friends, because she did like him now, ever since she had asked Jesus to help.

Playing the part of an angel in the Christmas program at school and wearing sparkling wings was great fun. Hilda also had to give a recitation at the church Christmas program, besides singing in the children's choir.

The church Christmas program was the biggest event of the season. Few families had Christmas trees in their own homes. The big Christmas tree at church belonged to everybody. Most people brought their family presents there to be handed out.

Mama couldn't go to the Christmas program. She didn't feel strong yet, and besides, Sigurd was too little to take out in the cold. She assured Hilda that she wouldn't mind missing it. She would have a peaceful Christmas at home with the baby.

Mama fixed Hilda's hair in French braids for the program and tied pink ribbons in her hair to go with the new blue dress she had sewed for her. Lois wore a green dress and had red ribbons on the ends of her long braids. John wore the suit Mama had made for him from an old one of Papa's. Hilda thought everyone looked fine.

Putting on their wraps, they waved goodbye to Mama and Sigurd and piled onto the sled.

Papa whistled Christmas carols all the way to the church, and sometimes Hilda hummed along. Otherwise, there were no sounds but the squeak of the sled runners on the snow. The snow that had seemed such an enemy to Hilda a few days before seemed like a friend now. How beautifully white it was, and how quickly the sled skimmed over it on their way to the long-awaited Christmas program.

Hilda's eyes grew big as she came into the church and saw the tall tree with tiny candles glowing all over it. It was so beautiful! There were bags under the tree for everyone. Hilda knew they were filled with candy, nuts, apples, and an orange.

Louise's mother bustled up to the front and placed some packages under the tree. Hilda felt a little pang of envy. Louise and her brothers and sisters always got a present under the tree

besides the bag of goodies. The Nelsons had more money than Papa did, though. She should be glad to get the bag of candy, nuts, and fruit and not wish for more.

Hilda's heart thumped wildly when it was her turn to give her recitation. The sea of faces before her almost made her forget her starting lines. Then she noticed Pete slouched in the back all by himself. Pete didn't know the true meaning of Christmas, because he didn't know Jesus. She would speak her recitation to him.

Hilda didn't forget a single word. She felt happy as she took her seat, glad she had done well and relieved that it was over. Now she could enjoy the rest of the program.

In between the recitations, the children's choir sang Christmas carols. Sometimes the audience joined in. At the very last, Pastor Lunde gave a short message.

"Remember whose birthday it is," he urged the people.

"It's Jesus' birthday, of course," mused Hilda. Then she gave a little gasp of dismay. She had no present for Jesus, and maybe nobody else had either. How would He feel on His birthday?

"Jesus said that when we do some kindness to someone else, it is the same as doing it to Him," explained the pastor. " 'Inasmuch as ye have done it unto one of the least of these my brethren, ye have done it unto me.' "

Hilda breathed a happy sigh of relief. Giving Pete the knife was the same, then, as giving a present to Jesus. It was her way of showing Jesus she loved Him and wanted to please Him. Hilda hugged herself happily. Christmas was such a wonderful time!

After the program, the young ladies of the church passed out the bags of goodies and the presents under the tree. Nels's older brother, Carl, and three other young men took turns watching the burning candles on the Christmas tree. They held long poles with a wet rag tied to the end. If a candle burned too low, they reached up with the long pole and put it out.

Hilda was so delighted with her bag of goodies, she hardly noticed what was going on around her until she heard Louise squeal with joy.

"Hilda, look! A doll! Mama and Papa gave me a doll for Christmas!"

"That's nice," said Hilda quietly, glancing at the doll. She couldn't bear to look too closely, not when she had never in her life had a store-bought doll, and this was Louise's third one.

Mama said she had planned to make new rag dolls for her and Lois, but little Sigurd arrived before he was expected, and after that she had no time. Oh, well, they had Sigurd. A real live baby was better than a doll, anyway, Hilda told herself.

Suddenly Hilda thought about Pete. Had he received their present yet? She turned around to look. As she did so, she heard someone call her name in front. She turned around quickly. Sophie Martin was looking for her.

"Oh, there you are," she said, handing her a long, narrow package.

"For me?" asked Hilda. "Are you sure?"

Sophie laughed. "Of course I'm sure. Unless there's another Hilda Johnson in our church that I don't know about."

Hilda looked at the package, too dazed to open it. Sure enough, it said, "Hilda Johnson, from Papa and Mama." How could Papa afford—? With trembling fingers, she opened the long box.

"A doll!" she cried out when she saw it. "A store-bought doll! A doll with a china head and real hair!" Oh, it was too wonderful to be true. Where was Lois? She must show her.

Lois, her eyes shining like stars, was pushing through the excited children to find Hilda. In her arms she, too, clasped a beautiful doll. Hilda's joy was complete.

The rest of the evening seemed like a dream. Hilda didn't even notice the cold as they rode home on the sled. Underneath the blankets, pressed close to her, was the wonderful doll, the first store-bought doll she had ever owned.

Lois was beside herself with joy for her doll. John was excited about the leather money purse Papa had bought for him. Papa was whistling Christmas carols. He hadn't received any present, but he seemed the happiest of all.

"How could you ever afford to buy us so much?" Hilda asked Papa, as they skimmed over the snow.

Papa chuckled. "I guess you'll have to thank your baby brother," he said. "Sigurd came before we could get the doctor. I didn't have to pay the doctor. That put us ahead a little bit."

Hilda heaved a happy sigh. All this and a baby brother besides! It was almost too good to be true.

Chapter 18
Papa's New Job

Papa came home from town one evening and announced he had gotten a job with the creamery for the remaining winter months. He and Mr. Peterson would haul blocks of ice from the lake to be stored and used in the summer for cooling milk and making ice cream.

Mama looked anxious. "Isn't that dangerous work, Henry?" she asked.

Papa stroked his beard. "Not as dangerous as staying home and getting in your way," he said with a chuckle.

Mama shook her head, pretending to be disgusted, but she was smiling.

Papa was happy about the creamery job. It was cold, hard work, but the extra money would come in handy.

"Maybe we can make the parlor bigger and add another bedroom to the house," he said.

"And get some linoleum for the parlor floor," Mama added.

Papa laughed. "Don't you be getting too many big ideas," he said. "I'll only be working two or three months."

One evening Papa wasn't home in time for supper.

"John, you run and do the chores," said Mama. "We'll keep supper until Papa comes. You help John, Hilda."

Papa still wasn't home when John and Hilda came back from the barn with the pail of milk. Mama was plainly worried.

"It's a dangerous job—taking ice from the lake. So easy to fall in, and the water so terribly cold." She walked back and forth across the kitchen floor, peering out of the window every few minutes.

"When are we going to eat?" asked Lois. "I'm hungry."

Mama stopped her pacing. "I guess we may as well eat," she said. "Hilda, help me dish up. John, you put up the chairs. We'll leave Papa's share in the warming oven."

Nobody spoke much at the table. Hilda felt afraid. Why was Papa so late? Had something terrible happened to him? Had he fallen into the icy water?

Voices! Stomping feet! Everybody jumped up joyfully and ran to the door. Mama opened the door and then put her hand to her mouth to

stifle a cry. Mr. Peterson and Dr. Ness were carrying Papa on a stretcher between them. His face was white and twisted with pain.

Mama shooed the children away to make room for the men with the stretcher. They carried Papa right into the bedroom and put him to bed as gently as possible. Mama went in after them. The doctor helped her take off Papa's outer clothes.

The children huddled near the door, whispering together in frightened tones.

"What happened to Papa?" asked Hilda, when Mama finally came out.

"He had a bad fall on the ice and hurt his back," she said. "He must lie very still until it heals." She went to the stove to warm up the coffee.

Dr. Ness came out of the bedroom and sat down by the table. Mama offered him supper, but he declined. "All I want is a cup of coffee—something to warm me up. I must be on my way."

Finishing the coffee in a few gulps, he stood up and wiped his mouth with his hanky. "If you nurse your husband as well as you did Hilda when she had smallpox, he'll soon be up and around again." He winked at Hilda. "I'll be back to check on him the day after tomorrow." The doctor went into the bedroom to get Mr. Peterson, and they were off.

Papa hurt too much to want to even talk the first few days, but after a while he felt better and asked Hilda to read to him when she came home from school. He especially liked to have Hilda read his Norwegian paper to him.

Dr. Ness came to see Papa often. Papa began to walk a little about the kitchen and try to sit. Little by little his back got better, but he still had some pain and couldn't work hard.

One day, Papa said to the children, "Mama and I have been talking about moving out west to Washington. I can't do heavy farm work anymore because of my back injury, but I may be able to handle light work in a factory. We are waiting for a letter from my cousin Ole, who lives in Bellingham.

Wails of protest greeted this announcement. "We don't want to move! We don't want to leave our farm!" Even John joined in. He had grown to like his new home almost as much as Hilda did.

"We must do what is best for Papa," answered Mama, quietly, as she picked up a half-finished stocking and started knitting.

The children didn't say more. Hilda felt dismayed. That night she couldn't go to sleep for a long time. What if they had to leave the farm, leave Minnesota, leave their friends and her maple tree? Just thinking about it made her feel sad and lonesome.

A week later, the long-awaited letter from Bellingham, Washington, arrived. Cousin Ole said Papa could get a job in the pulp mill. Ole was a foreman and had something to say about who should be hired.

"You'd like it here," he wrote. "The country resembles Norway. There are mountains and evergreen trees. The ocean is nearby for deep-sea fishing. The climate is mild. We have had some snow this year, but some winters we get hardly any, and it doesn't last long if we do. In the summer there is an abundance of berries and fruit."

Papa's eyes shone as he read the letter to the family. "Well, Magda, what do you say?" he asked.

Mama's mouth was set in a firm line. Hilda had the feeling she didn't want to leave for a strange place, either. "We can't go unless we sell the farm," she said.

"You're right," agreed Papa, stroking his beard thoughtfully. "And winter is not a good time to sell."

Hilda breathed a sigh of relief. If they couldn't sell the farm, they couldn't move to Washington. They would have to stay. Maybe John could do the farm work and Hilda could help. Hilda never, never wanted to leave the farm where her special maple tree stood and where she had so many happy memories!

Hilda wished she could climb up her maple tree right now and talk to God about this new problem, but it was much too cold. Instead, she ran upstairs and knelt beside her bed.

"Please, please, God," she pleaded, "don't let Papa sell the farm."

Chapter 19
To the Mountain

Papa did sell the farm. Mr. Peterson's nephew from Indiana wanted to start farming in Minnesota, and a farm located right next to his uncle's was just what he had been looking for.

Hilda couldn't believe it. Why hadn't God answered her prayer?

Hilda remembered another prayer of hers that God hadn't answered the way she wanted him to. That was the one about the new Mama. The new Mama had come in spite of Hilda's prayer that she wouldn't. Now Hilda was glad she had. She couldn't imagine how it would be not to have Mama and John around. Yes, she had to admit that God knew best when He said "No" to her prayer not to send them.

But selling the farm—that was another matter. That just *couldn't* be good. Could it?

Papa whistled a lot these days. He seemed happy to be moving away from the farm. Hilda didn't see how he could be.

"I can't see why you're so happy about leaving the farm," she said to him crossly one morning.

Papa stopped whistling and drew her to his knee. It had been a long time since Hilda had sat on Papa's knee.

"My dear girl," he said, "I am happy because

God is taking care of us. How could we stay on the farm when I cannot do farm work anymore? God has given me a different job that I can handle, and I am very thankful to Him. It makes a man happy when he knows he can support his family.''

Hilda studied her fingernails thoughtfully. "I see, Papa," she answered softly at last.

"The Bible says that 'All things work together for good to them that love God,'" went on Papa. "He must have some purpose for our moving to Washington, because of the way He let things work out. Let's be happy about it and thankful."

"All right, Papa." Hilda slipped off Papa's knee and ran to get ready for school. Today she must tell Louise that Papa had sold the farm, but somehow after what Papa had said it wouldn't be quite so hard.

A week later, Miss Dahlen and the children at school had a farewell party for Hilda and John. Then the church held a special potluck supper to honor the Johnson family before they left. Friends came to say goodbye and brought gifts. Hilda helped Mama pack. At last the day came for them to leave.

Hilda got up early, dressed warmly, and ran out to the maple tree. She couldn't keep from crying, as she knew it would be the last time with her tree. She had talked to God so many times here. Would life ever be the same without her maple tree?

Hilda couldn't climb the tree, because the snow around it was too deep, but at least she could look at it and say goodbye. With a last fond glance, and wiping away a few tears, she ran back to the house, where preparations for leaving were in full swing.

The next two hours passed quickly. A last tearful look around the old home. A last glimpse of her maple tree from her seat on top of the baggage on the Petersons' sleigh. Breakfast at Petersons'. Friends at the depot. Tearful hugs and goodbyes. And at last they were on the train.

The train pulled slowly out of the station. Hilda waved to her friends on the platform until she could see them no more. Then she settled down on the green, plush seat beside Lois with her doll clasped in her arms. John had fixed his seat so it faced theirs. Papa and Mama sat in the one across the aisle, and little Sigurd slept peacefully on Mama's lap.

At first, nobody spoke; they all just looked in wonder out the window. It seemed to Hilda that the fields were moving, not the train. She watched, fascinated.

"Oh, I almost forgot," said John at last, digging in his pocket. "Pete told me to give you this." He pulled a little package out of his pocket and handed it to Hilda.

Hilda took it gingerly. She remembered the cow's tail and all the other mean tricks Pete had played on her. Did she dare open it?

"Open it!" said John.

Cautiously, Hilda tore away the brown paper, expecting the worst. Then she gave a little gasp of surprise. There lay the hanky she had lost at the missionary picnic, with pennies tied in one corner! Hilda untied the knot and counted them: "One, two, three, four, five, six, seven." She looked up at John with shining eyes. "I lost only five, but he gave me seven!" she exclaimed.

"I think the two extra ones mean that he's sorry," remarked John.

Hilda carefully tied up the pennies in the hanky again and put them in the new pocketbook Mrs.

Peterson had given her. She had a warm feeling inside. Pete was her friend at last.

The hours passed quickly, and soon it was time to eat the lunch Mrs. Peterson had prepared for them: buns with slices of roast pork, jelly sandwiches, an apple for each, chocolate cake, and even some lefsa left over from the church farewell party.

John grew restless after they had eaten, and he walked up and down the aisle of the car, but Hilda was content to sit and watch the scenery fly by.

The clickety-clack of the train wheels and the clang of the cars banging against one another finally lulled Hilda to sleep. She didn't wake up until darkness had fallen. At first, she didn't realize where she was. Then she looked around at her sleeping family and remembered. Papa was even snoring a little.

Hilda propped her doll up on the seat; then, turning towards the window, she placed her arms on the sill and looked out. The hills were bigger now, and there behind them all, right underneath a gleaming star, Hilda saw something she had never seen before—a mountain. She gasped with pleasure as she pressed her nose against the window to get a better look.

The mountain seemed to beckon to Hilda. It seemed to say, "Come and learn new things and have new adventures in new places."

Suddenly, Hilda was glad she was on her way to Washington, even if it had been hard to leave her home and friends. She looked at the mountain and the star and silently breathed a prayer of thanks.

"Dear God, I'm so glad I can have my best Friend with me always. I didn't have to leave *You* back there in the maple tree. You will go with me into the mountains, too!"

The train wheels went clickety-clack, clickety-clack. Hilda felt content and happy. She didn't know what lay beyond the mountain, but somehow she was sure it would be something good.

GLOSSARY

The following glossary to *Secret in the Maple Tree* helps you understand the story better. Words from the story that may be hard for you are listed in alphabetical order. The glossary helps you sound out the words and understand their meaning in the story. If you need help on a word that is not in the glossary, use your classroom dictionary. The pronunciation key below will help you to pronounce the words.

Pronunciation Key

Symbol	Example	Symbol	Example	Symbol	Example
ā	āte	ē̃	makē̃r	o͝o	bo͝ok
â	dâre	ī	īce	ou	out
ă	făt	ĭ	ĭt	th	there
ȧ	pȧth	i	anĭmal	tu̇	pictu̇re
ä	fäther	ō	ōver	ū	ūnit
a	loyal	o̊	o̊bey	u̇	u̇nited
ə	ago (ə · gō)	ô	côrd	û	hûrt
ē	ēven	o̧	so̧ft	ŭ	ŭp
e̊	be̊tween	ŏ	nŏt	u	focus
ĕ	ĕgg	oi	boil		
e	recent	o͞o	fo͞od		

142

A

a·bun·dance (a·bŭn′dăns)
  a great plenty

al·bum (ăl′bum) a book for
  pictures

anx·ious·ly (ăngk′shus·lĭ) with a
  feeling of worry

ar·ti·cle (är′tĭ·k'l) a thing of a par-
  ticular kind

as·ton·ish (as·tŏn′ĭsh) to surprise

auc·tion (ôk′shun) a public sale to
  the highest bidder

auc·tion·eer (ôk′shun·ēr′) a
  person who sells at an auction

B

ba·sin (bā′s'n) a pan for water

bat·ter (băt′ĕr) to beat
  repeatedly with violence

beck·on (bĕk′un) to call

be·wil·der (bĕ·wĭl′dĕr) to con-
  fuse

bliz·zard (blĭz′ĕrd) a severe and
  long snowstorm

blonde (blŏnd) light-colored

blur (blûr) to grow hazy

bou·quet (bō·kā′) a bunch of
  flowers

brim·ming (brĭm′ĭng) about to
  overflow

brisk (brĭsk) lively

143

C

can (kăn) to preserve food by putting it in sealed cans or jars

catch·y (kăch′ĭ) easily remembered

churn (chûrn) to stir cream to make butter

clench (klĕnch) to close tightly

cob·web (kŏb′wĕb) a spider's web

com·i·cal (kŏm′ĭ·kɑl) funny

com·mu·ni·ty (ko·mū′ni·tĭ) a neighborhood

com·pete (kom·pēt′) to have a contest

coop (kōōp) a chicken house

co·zy (kō′zĭ) snug

cream·er·y (krēm′ẽr·ĭ) a dairy

cup·board (kŭb′ẽrd) a place for keeping dishes

cy·clone (sī′klōn) a tornado; a fierce windstorm

D

de·cent (dē′sent) fairly good

de·pot (dē′pō) a railroad station

de·spite·ful (dĕ·spīt′fo͞ol) cruel

de·vo·tion (dĕ·vō′shun) private
  worship

dis·ease (dĭ·zēz′) sickness

dis·may (dĭs·mā′)
  disappointment

dis·miss (dĭs·mĭs′) to send
  away

dox·ol·o·gy (dŏks·ŏl′ŏ·jĭ)
  a short hymn of praise

drift (drĭft) snow that is piled
  together in a heap by the wind

E

E·li·jah (ĕ·lī′jȧ) one of the Old
  Testament prophets

elm (ĕlm) a large tree that is
  planted for shade

en·coun·ter (ĕn·koun′tẽr) a
  meeting

en·vy (ĕn′vĭ) jealousy

er·rand (ĕr′and) a special trip

e·ter·nal (ĕ·tûr′nal) forever

ex·pose (ĕks·pōz′) to leave
  unprotected

F

flat·i·ron (flăt′ī′ẽrn) an iron
  with a flat, smooth surface,
  that is heated in a fire
for·eign (fŏr′ĭn) a country
  other than our own
for·lorn (fŏr·lŏrn′) unhappy
fra·grant (frā′grant) agree-
  able in smell
fret (frĕt) to worry

G

germ (jûrm) a cause of disease
gin·ger·ly (jĭn′jẽr·lĭ) with great
  caution
glum (glŭm) sullen; sad and silent
gran·a·ry (grăn′ə·rĭ) a
  storehouse for grain
grove (grōv) a small group of trees
grub (grŭb) food
grum·bly (grŭm′blĭ) bad-
  tempered
guilt·y (gĭl′tĭ) having done
  wrong
guz·zle (gŭz′′l) to drink quickly

H

hank·y (hăng′kĭ) a handkerchief

har·ness (här′nĕs) the gear of a horse

hay·mow (hā′·mou′) the part of a barn where hay is kept

hea·then (hē′then) not a Christian

herd (hûrd) to keep together

hitch (hĭch) to fasten on

hum·ding·er (hŭm′ding′ẽr) something that is very unusual

I

Il·li·nois (ĭl′i·noi′) one of the states of the United States of America

ILLINOIS

in·fect (ĭn·fĕkt′) to cause disease

in·sult (ĭn·sŭlt′) to offend by word or deed

in·tend (ĭn·tĕnd′) to plan to do something

in·ter·fer·ence (ĭn′tẽr·fẽr′ens) getting in the way of

J

jack·knife (jăk′nīf) a large
  pocket knife

K

ker·o·sene (kĕr′ō·sēn′) a thin
  mineral oil used for burning
  in lamps

L

lean-to (lēn′tōō) an added shed
lef·sa (lĕf′sə) a Norwegian dessert
  made with mashed potatoes and
  flour
li·no·le·um (lĭ·nō′lĕ·um) a kind
  of floor covering
luke·warm (lūk′wôrm′) neither
  hot nor cold

M

ma·ple (mā′p′l) a hardwood
  tree
mea·sles (mē′z′lz) a disease

Min·ne·ap·o·lis
(mĭn′ē·ăp′ō·lĭs) the largest
city in Minnesota

Min·ne·so·ta (mĭn′ē·sō′tə) one
of the states of the United
States of America.

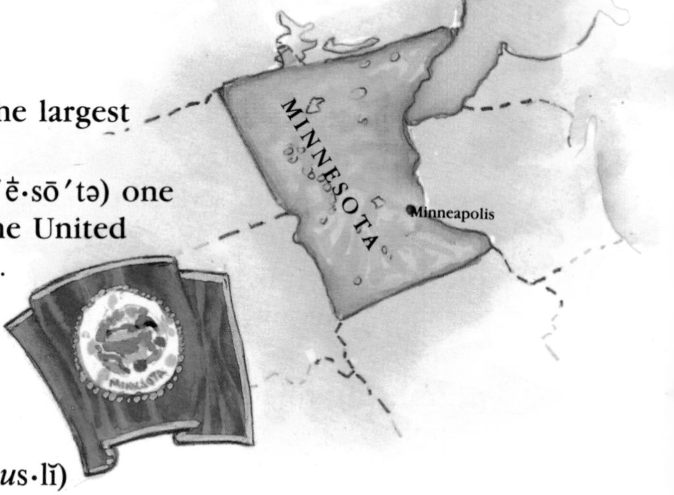

N

nerv·ous·ly (nûr′vus·lĭ)
fearfully

non·sense (nŏn′sĕns)
foolishness

Nor·way (nôr′wā) a country of
northern Europe

numb·ness (nŭm′nĕs) without
feeling

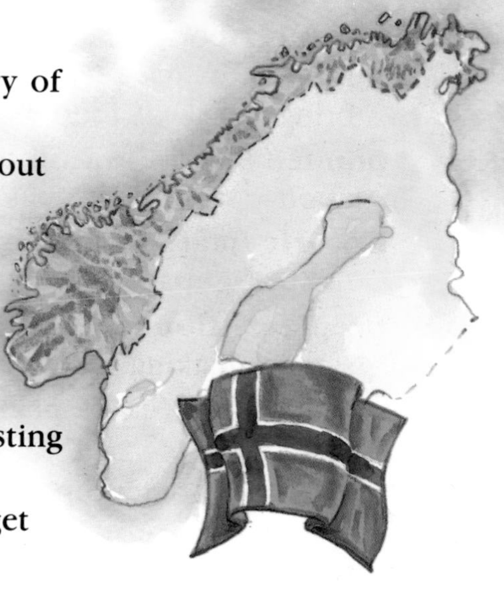

O

out·burst (out′bûrst) a bursting
forth of strong feelings

out·smart (out·smärt′) to get
the better of

P

par·lor (pär′lĕr) a living room

part·ner (pärt′nĕr) one who
has a part in something with
another

pas·ture (pàs′t̯ụ̈r) grassland for grazing animals

perch (pûrch) a place of rest

per·se·cute (pûr′sĕ̈·kūt) to cause to suffer

pic·nick·er (pĭk′nĭk·ẽr) a person who enjoys a meal in the open air

plumb·ing (plŭm′ĭng) water pipes

poi·son (poi′z′n) a substance causing illness or death when eaten or drunk

pot·luck (pŏt′lŭk) an informal meal to which several families bring a dish of food

pounce (pouns) to rush down upon

prai·rie (prâr′ĭ) a meadow or tract of grassland

prep·a·ra·tion (prĕp′ə·rā′-shun) a making ready

pro·ject (prŏj′ĕkt) a planned task

proph·et (prŏf′ĕt) one who speaks for God

ℛ

ras·cal (răs′kal) a mean, trickish fellow; a dishonest person

re·ar·range (rē′a·rānj′) to put into another order

rec·i·ta·tion (rĕs′i·tā′·shun) the delivery before an audience of something committed to memory

ref·uge (rĕf′ūj) a shelter

rein (rān) the strap of a bridle used by a rider to guide a horse

rel·ish (rĕl′ĭsh) to enjoy

re·quire (rĕ·kwīr′) to demand

res·cue (rĕs′kū) deliverance

re·sem·ble (rĕ·zĕm′b′l) to be like or similar to

re·tort (rĕ·tôrt′) a quick, sharp reply

rhu·barb (rōō′bärb) a garden plant

S

saun·ter (sôn′tēr) to walk lazily

scowl (skoul) to look angry

scur·ry (skûr′ĭ) to hasten quickly

shim·mer (shĭm′ēr) to glimmer

slough (slou) a wet place

small·pox (smôl′pŏks′) a disease

smirk (smûrk) a sly smile

sneer (snēr) to smile with a look which shows scorn

snick·er (snĭk′ēr) to giggle

som·er·sault (sŭm′ēr·sôlt) a turning end over end

spar·kling (spär′klĭng) glittering

squawk (skwôk) a harsh sound

stan·chion (stăn′shun) wooden bars used to secure a cow's head while it is being milked

stealth·i·ly (stĕl′thĭ·lĭ) slyly

stern (stûrn) harsh

sti·fle (stī′f'l) to stop

stin·gy (stĭn′jĭ) selfish

stout·ly (stout′lĭ) without yielding

stretch·er (strĕch′ẽr) a board used for carrying a person

styl·ish (stīl′ĭsh) in fashion

sulk (sŭlk) to be silent and bad-tempered

sul·try (sŭl′trĭ) very hot and moist

sus·pi·cion (sus·pĭsh′un) without trust

swoop (swo͞op) to pounce upon and grab

T

thim·ble (thĭm′b'l) a kind of cap used in sewing to pro-

152

tect the finger when pushing
the needle through the
material

thresh (thrĕsh) to beat out
grain

tor·ment (tôr′mĕnt) to cause
suffering

tor·rent (tôr′ent) a downpour

tramp (trămp) a foot-traveler
who usually begs for a living

twine (twīne) to twist together

U

u·ni·son (ū′ni·sun) sounding
together

V

va·cant (vā′kant) empty

vac·ci·nate (văk′si·nāt) to
protect from disease by
inoculation

W

wid·ow (wĭd′ō) a woman
whose husband has died

Will·mar (wĭl′mẽr) a city in
Minnesota

wist·ful (wĭst′foŏl) longing

wob·bly (wŏb′lĭ) unsteady